One Night with
a Hero

a Heroes novel

Laura Kaye

Entangled Publishing, LLC
2614 South Timberline Road
Suite 109
Fort Collins, CO 80525
Visit our website at www.entangledpublishing.com.

Brazen is an imprint of Entangled Publishing, LLC. For more information on our titles, visit www.brazenbooks.com.

Edited by Heather Howland
Cover design by Heather Howland
Cover art by Shutterstock

Manufactured in the United States of America

First Edition October 2012

To all the everyday heroes,
thank you for all you do.

Thank you for acting despite your fear.
Thank you for serving with no expectation of reward.
Thank you for helping because it's right.
Thank you for inspiring each and every one of us.

Chapter One

Brady Scott ran down the Mount Vernon trail, the breeze off the Potomac River offering little relief from the late afternoon sun. The rush of blood through his ears, the rhythmic dull thud of silenced dog tags against his bare chest, the constant overhead roar of airplanes landing at Reagan National Airport—none of it was any use. He couldn't get the therapist's most recent assignment out of his head.

Get closure with your father.

Stationed back in the country three months with orders to get his head on straight if he wanted to go up for promotion, and it all came down to daddy issues.

Son of a bitch.

As if it wasn't bad enough being forced to see a therapist. There was no making yourself okay with the things Joseph Scott had done. Every mark Brady's little sister, Alyssa, had worn on her skin, every tear she'd spilled in fright, every wide-eyed *help me* gaze she'd ever thrown his way had sliced into Brady's heart until he was certain it lay shredded in his chest. He'd been old enough to fight back and defend himself, but Alyssa never stood a chance against their dad.

His stomach soured and churned at the memories. If that was the shit "love" led to, he wanted no part of it, thank you very much.

The trail dumped him into Old Town Alexandria, which was nicer for the shade the buildings and trees along Union Street provided, but more challenging for the crowds of people that thronged the sidewalks, and the rush of traffic that paid no heed to pedestrians. Brady bit out a curse as he dodged a minivan circling for parking and crossed the street, where the sidewalk brought him along Founders Park, a long strip of green that bordered Alexandria's waterfront. The park was crowded with groups staking out real estate in the grass with lawn chairs, blankets, and coolers.

Brady slowed to a jog, then to a walk as he came up behind a family pushing a stroller. "What's going on tonight?"

The father glanced at Brady's ID tags and gave him a smile. "Labor Day fireworks at sunset."

"Oh, yeah?" He was halfway through the ten-mile trail he'd sketched out. Maybe he'd come back down after grabbing a quick shower. Assuming he could find towels. And the shower curtain. He hadn't exactly unpacked after moving in to his new town house last night. And then it had been the ass crack of dawn before he'd gotten home from celebrating his new digs with the guys.

He was about to kick it back into a run when he saw her.

A woman sitting on a blanket removed from the mass of people. Arms around her knees, chin resting on an arm, forgotten book at her side.

She was all long lines and sun-kissed skin, and Brady couldn't stop looking. Wavy dark hair twisted on top of her head. A wide-necked white shirt exposed a long column of throat and most of one shoulder. Crossed at the ankles, the part of her legs not covered by the long skirt were tanned and toned.

Love, he wanted no part of. Lust, however, was a welcome old friend.

His mind churning on a plan, he braced his hands on his hips and debated how to approach her.

Her gaze swung around. Brady sucked in a breath. He would've thought those green eyes the most beautiful he'd ever seen, if they hadn't been glassy with tears. She blinked and looked away.

His brain shifted gears and he walked toward her before he'd even thought to do it, concern a growing weight on his chest and anger at whoever hurt her searing his gut. Neither made any sense, really, but he never could stand to see a girl cry. Hell, that instinct went way back. "Hey, you all right?"

She cast him a sidelong glance. "Peachy, thanks."

What's the attitude for? Caught off guard by the sarcasm in her tone, he dragged a hand through his hair and noticed hers had pink highlights mixed in with the rich brown. "Uh—"

"Look." Her grip tightened around her knees. "I appreciate the Good Samaritan routine and all, but I'm not looking for a hero today. Capisce?"

The hard edge to her tone was full of stubbornness and challenge. So much for trying to be the good guy. "Capisce? Seriously? Did we just step into *The Godfather* and I didn't know it?"

She rose in one fluid movement and brushed at the thin colorful skirt, a wrist full of bracelets jingling as she moved. A cascade of stars tattooed the skin behind a heavily pierced ear. "And what's wrong with *The Godfather*? It's one of the top ten movies of all time."

He drank in all her details, assessing and weighing her as if she were any other adversary he'd determined to figure out. About his age, he'd guess. "You like *The Godfather*?"

Standing on the edge of her blanket, she gave him a once-over that made his bare skin go hot. "Yeah. And what of it, sailor?"

He narrowed his gaze, his internal temperature kicking up another few degrees. "I got no beef with *The Godfather*, but I'm not a sailor." Fuckin' A, he couldn't tell if they were fighting or flirting, but these running shorts were about to make it crystal clear his body believed it was the latter.

She shook her head and looked at him, all hint of those tears long gone, the bright green of her eyes still stunning. In bare feet, she stepped into the grass and closed the four-foot gap between them. Brady's gaze was torn between watching her curvy body move and reading the ink that decorated the side of her foot. Her body won out, the way the thin cotton shirt shaped around her full breasts capturing his attention. She stopped in front of him, and his body went on alert, shoulders tense and muscles tight—not out of fear, but out of anticipation. The tats, the piercings, the hard wariness in her gaze, and the challenging tilt to her chin gave her a tough edge that was just shy of beautiful, but man was he was more than sold.

She flicked at his ID tags with her fingers and arched a brow. "I can see that."

The army was the only service that didn't spell out its acronym on the tags. Someone knew her military trivia. A fact that made her equal parts more interesting and more annoying. "Which is why you said it."

She licked her lips. "Now you're getting the picture."

Jesus, her tongue was pierced. Could this chick get any hotter? He wanted to pull her in and see if that mouth tasted as sweet as it looked. And bonus that it would cut off the stream of sarcasm she'd been dishing out. He tucked his hands in his pockets and chuffed out a humorless laugh. "Why are you messing with me?"

She pressed those ruby reds together, turning the smile he could've sworn she'd almost given him into a smirk. "Because you're an easy target."

"*I'm* an easy target? I think you have me confused with some other squid." Five years in the Army Special Forces, and Brady hadn't suffered a single injury. An easy target was the last thing he was. Not all his buddies had been so lucky, though, like his best friend, Marco. A good guy through and through, and yet he'd been injured so severely he'd been medically discharged and still struggled with his recovery—all while someone like *Brady* got off without a scratch. How fucking fair was that? His fists curled and he clamped down on the anger his thoughts unleashed.

"Nope. Just talking about you." Without a backward glance, she returned to her blanket. Damn if that skirt didn't hint at the very fine smart-ass beneath.

Brady shifted to hide his body's reaction to her, sure she was going to look his way again, but she didn't. She stretched out on her stomach, kicked her ankles up, and crossed them—revealing more leg in the process as her skirt pooled behind her knees—and grabbed her book.

Dis-missed. *Damn.*

What-the-fuck-ever. He scrubbed his hand over his short hair and after a moment of indecision, made for the brick sidewalk. When was the last time he'd been turned on, pissed off, amused, and embarrassed all at the same time? Being in her presence was like riding a roller coaster in the dark, totally unaware of whether a hill, a sharp turn, or a frickin' free fall was coming at you next.

"Hey, sailor boy?"

"Son of a…," he said under his breath, turning despite himself. He met her amused gaze. She freaking knew she had him in knots. "Yeah?"

Her expression changed, grew more serious. "Just… thanks for asking."

His heart kicked up in his chest. She could be vulnerable, too, and that gave him hope. "You got it, Pinky."

She wrinkled her nose. "Seriously?"

He smirked and found himself walking toward her again. She'd taken the bait just like he'd hoped she would. "Don't like the nickname? Gimme your real name instead." He crossed his arms and watched an array of expressions pass over her face.

She pretended disinterest and returned her focus to her open book, which—*ding ding ding, now we're talking*—was upside down in her hands.

He crouched down in front of her and grabbed the book. "It might help"—he made a big show of turning the book right side up and placing it back in her fingers—"if you read it this way."

Laughter spilled out of her and she dropped her face

behind the open pages, shoulders shaking. The sound was deep and throaty, and the tension melted out of Brady's neck. Finally, she glanced back up, smiling so freely all the toughness fell away, leaving an exotically beautiful woman. If Brady hadn't been hooked before, wanting to hear that sound and see that smile shape those full, dark red lips reeled him right in. It was an odd reaction for him, which made her a particularly good distraction. She'd kept him guessing more than anyone he'd met in a long time.

He tapped his fingers against the back of the book. "Name."

The woman grinned up at him for a long moment, then rolled her eyes, which lingered on his bare chest.

Brady arched an eyebrow. "*Name*."

She heaved a sigh like she was all put out. "Joss."

"Joss. Okay. See, that wasn't so hard, was it? I'm Brady."

Joss pushed into a sitting position and tucked her legs under the pink-and-green tie-dyed skirt. The tattoo on her foot he'd glimpsed earlier read "courage" in elegant script. Now he was not only attracted, but intrigued. This chick was pushing all his buttons.

She tossed her book to the blanket. "Anyone ever tell you you're kind of a pain in the ass, Brady?"

He managed a rueful grin. "Every damn day."

"And why is it you sound so proud of that fact?"

He held out his hands and shrugged. "We all have to excel at something."

She tried to rein in her smile. Failed. "Congratulations, then, I guess?"

"Thanks." He glanced over his shoulder, toward where the grass was filling with people waiting for the evening's show, then looked back to her. "You gonna stay for the fireworks?"

"That was the plan."

"Good. So, pizza, sub sandwiches, or fried chicken?"

"Excuse me?"

"Which one would you prefer I bring back for dinner?"

More of that free laughter spilled from her lips, making a big old show out of her tongue piercing. Man how he'd love a closer inspection of that little silver ball. She shook her head. "You're not serious."

"As a heart attack."

"Okay, well. On the *off chance* you actually come back, surprise me."

Brady rose and patted his hand twice over his heart. "Oh, you can count on that. Gimme an hour, ninety minutes tops."

"Right on, sailor boy."

He shook his head. "Before the night's through, we're gonna cure you of that," he said, then he turned, hit the sidewalk, and broke into run. All those dark thoughts of his father he hadn't been able to shake earlier? They were long gone.

Chapter Two

Jocelyn Daniels watched the man make his way through the tourists until she couldn't see him—or his powerful thighs and incredibly well-muscled back—anymore.

Well, that was interesting.

Shaking her head, she stretched out on her blanket. Maybe she should go home. Not because she believed the guy would return, but because her emotions were clearly too close to the surface for public consumption. If only she hadn't run into Ethan and his freaking new girlfriend at the store this morning.

Apparently it was just *her* he wasn't ready to commit to. Because the woman's round belly and glittering ring finger sure as hell looked like commitment to Jocelyn.

It would be really nice if, just once, someone wanted to keep her.

So not helpful, Joss. Cut it out. But she couldn't help it. Seeing Ethan happily devoted to another woman seemed further proof that men would always leave her.

She sighed and tucked a loose strand of hair behind her ear.

To be honest, though, she felt a lot better after the run-in with Brady. He'd been an unexpected distraction. And it never hurt to be flirted with, especially when the guy was so…really, really freaking hot. And funny. And kind of annoyingly endearing.

Yeah. That definitely explained her lighter mood.

She retrieved her novel, her gaze going unfocused as she remembered the embarrassment of being caught holding it upside down. Thank God he hadn't noticed what it was about. She hid her growing smile behind the book, her mind going back to the sight of him.

Sailor boy. The nickname tugged at Joss's cheeks. Tall. Built. Light-brown hair kissed by the sun with a hint of blond. All that lean, bare muscle. The way his running shorts had hung low enough to reveal the cut of his hips. Sex on a freaking stick.

And a soldier to boot. Bet he looked seriously fine in his dress uniform. Panties probably dropped at the mere sight—thongs, too. Maybe even like the one she was currently wearing.

Not that she was actually expecting Brady to return and put her willpower to the test. And that was for the best. Because she suspected he would be a little too much fun to play with and a lot too risky for her fragile ego. Her thong should have nothing to worry about.

Something bumped into her arm, pulling Joss from her thoughts. She glanced up into the smiling eyes of a toddler retrieving a pink plastic ball that had rolled onto her blanket.

"Hi, sweetie. Is this yours?"

The little girl with a yellow gingham jumper pointed. "Ball."

A woman came jogging over. "I'm sorry."

"Oh, it's all right. Here you go." She held the ball out and the girl took it in her chubby hands.

"Thanks." The mom smiled and playfully tugged on the girl's blond pigtail. "Come on, Emily."

"Ball!" the girl shouted, holding it up to her mother.

"That's right," the woman said.

Joss watched them return to their neighboring blanket, an empty ache forming in her chest. The girl threw the ball in the air and chased it when it bounced.

One day, that would be her. A wife, a mom, having a fun outing with her family. It wasn't the kind of dream people expected she'd embrace from looking at her. Nothing said June Cleaver like tattoos, piercings, and pink highlights, right? But the two had more in common than was obvious on the surface. When you grew up alone in the world without a family, you had to carve out your own identity. The ink and metal coloring and piercing her skin told the story of that effort, but they didn't mean she still didn't yearn for the family.

She sighed and opened her book again. The badass, hard-bodied Navy SEAL in this story rocked her world. Only now, she couldn't help but imagine a certain flirtatious soldier in the hero's place. That didn't hurt one bit.

Soon, the words sucked her in, drew her into a battle scene with a bad guy that made her forget the sun and breeze and growing crowd. Having spent so much time alone, reading had always been her biggest source of escape. When she read, she lost track of what was happening around her. Many times in her life, that had been a damn good thing.

Which is why she didn't hear him.

"That must be some good book," a loud—and amused—male voice said.

Joss looked up into Brady's smiling brown eyes. "Oh," she said. "Were you…I didn't…you're back."

He smiled, and she shook off the story's hold on her, surprised to see that the sun was much lower in the sky and park grounds more filled with people. "You doubted me?"

She pushed into a sitting position and drank him in. The gray T-shirt emphasized the hard expanse of his chest and the warmth of his tan, and the khaki cargo shorts allowed her to catch a glimpse of those cut calf muscles again. She worked her gaze up to his face and found him watching her with a smug smile.

Heat roared over her cheeks. "Yeah, I guess I did."

She eyed the pizza box and brown paper bag in his hands, her heartbeat kicking up in her chest. This guy was ten kinds of damn hot. And he came bearing gifts. Kind of an irresistible combination. "So, what did you bring me?"

"Does that mean I can sit down?"

She bit back a smile. "I suppose."

Brady placed the food on the blanket and settled himself next to her. He flipped open the box lid. "Half cheese, half pepperoni." From the bag, he pulled paper plates, two bottles of water, two bags of chips, and two sandwiches wrapped in white butcher paper. "One turkey and cheese, one Italian."

Forget the food. Joss swallowed the moan she nearly uttered as the breeze kicked up and his scent surrounded her—all fresh soap and clean male. She shook her head and surveyed the feast. "Wow. Thank you. This is enough to feed an army."

He shrugged and gave her what was almost a sheepish smile, and Joss's stomach flipped at the appearance of this aw-shucks-good-guy persona, so different from the cocky bad boy he'd mostly shown her so far. "Wanted to be sure there was something here you'd like."

Oh, she was in so much trouble. This guy was not only handsome and dangerously charming, but considerate, too. And going way out of his way, for her. "Well, I like everything I see," she said, embracing a bit of brazenness even as her heart fluttered in her chest.

Brady cocked an eyebrow, his brown eyes sparkling with mischief. "Do ya, now?"

She held his gaze for a long moment, heat and competitiveness roaring between them. Finally, she looked away and reached for a bottle of water. He let out an infuriatingly smug chuckle and leaned forward to get it for her. Their hands touched on the bottle. The warmth of his skin sent tingles up her arm and shot her heart into a full-on sprint. His tongue stroked over his lower lip and Joss was suddenly *starving*, but not for the picnic in front of them.

Wow, this guy was like sexual Red Bull.

Not to mention Ethan had never elicited the wild desire now pounding through Joss's body, and Brady had barely touched her. Not that there would be touching.

Right. No touching. Absolutely not.

He smirked and grabbed his bottle, taking a long drink that made the knot in his throat bob until she had to look away to restrain the urge to feel the movement with her tongue. Geez, even the chunky black watch on his wrist was sexy. She twisted the cap and tilted the water to her lips. The coolness soothed the heat racking her body.

Get a freaking grip, Joss.

"So, what's your pleasure?"

She cut her gaze to him, forcing a swallow down. He gestured to the food, but that sparkle was there in his eyes again. Her brain raced on the possible ways she might find pleasure with him. "I'll start with the pizza," she managed to say.

They dished out the food, two slices for her, one slice and half of the Italian sandwich for him. As they made small talk, she inhaled the pizza, not realizing how hungry she'd been until she started to eat. The crust had just the right crunch to it, the sauce just the right spice. Delicious.

"There's something about having a picnic that makes the food taste better," she said as she took a small third slice of pizza.

"I've eaten plenty of meals outside that weren't as nice as this. I think it's the company more than the location." He popped open a bag of chips and extended it toward her.

She reached in and retrieved a handful, not sure why she'd accepted when she was getting so full. *Because you can't say no to him, especially when he's being all…cute and… charming. You. Are. In. So. Much. Trouble.* "Thanks," she said. Caught in a moment of awkwardness, Joss sipped at her water. "So, uh…" She scrambled for a topic. "Do you run a lot?"

He shrugged. "Most days."

That sure explained his body, which radiated power and leashed strength even as he relaxed next to her. "I really suck at running."

Brady gave her the closest thing to a full smile she'd seen. And damn if it wasn't endearing, especially with the way his eyes crinkled at the corners. "Why do you say that?"

"Because I do. I feel like I'm dying after about five minutes. I don't know how you do it."

He wiped his mouth with the napkin, then stuffed it in the bag with the rest of his trash. "I thought I was in shape when I entered basic training. First PT run—what you just said? That was exactly how I felt. I think I only got through it because my buddy hauled my ass the last mile. That and my drill sergeant might've been the devil."

She chuckled, getting reeled in a little bit more by his self-deprecation when undoubtedly he no longer had that problem. And probably never did. "Nothing like the devil to make you haul ass, huh?"

"That's the damn truth. So, are you sated yet?"

"What?"

He quirked a crooked grin. "All done?"

He pointed to the spread in front of them, but Joss had enough experience to recognize a smooth talker when she saw one. "You playing with me?"

"No, ma'am." He nailed her with a serious expression. "Not yet."

Heat roared over her cheeks. How he managed to infuse that military politeness she loved into something so laden with innuendo she had no idea. But the tingles skittering over her skin sure meant she liked it. She chuffed out a laugh. "Bad, bad news," she muttered.

"What's that?"

"Nothing you need to know, sailor boy." She looked at him from under her lashes to make sure he knew she was just riding him. Her hands fumbled the trash she was gathering as an arresting image gripped her—her, *riding him*, as in… *Geez, Joss. There will be no riding. Get. A. Grip.*

Why not? an insidious little voice whispered.

She released a shaky breath and busied her hands with the trash. "I am done. Thanks a lot for bringing all this. Can I give you some money for it?"

"Not a chance. You provided the blanket. I provided the food. We're square." He pushed the leftover food to the side and collected the trash. "Be right back."

It was damn near impossible to drag her gaze away from his ass as he maneuvered between the blankets and chairs to the trash can, but she needed to do something before he returned. She grabbed her phone and sent her best friend a text message.

> *Met someone named Brady at fireworks. Just talking. But if you don't hear from me by midnight have the police look for my body parts at Founders Park. :P*

Brady settled down beside her.

She dropped her phone into her lap. "So, how long are you stationed in the area?"

He braced his forearms on his knees. "Two years, give or take. Working for the Army Staff at the Pentagon."

"Oh, that sounds interesting. And where were you before here?" Her phoned beeped.

"Stationed out of Okinawa, but lots of places from there."

"You could tell me but then you'd have to kill me?"

He smirked. "Something like that."

"How long have you been in?"

"A little over five years." He fingered a design in the condensation on his bottle of water. "What do you do?"

Her phone beeped again. "I help run a community center for disadvantaged kids."

"Yeah? Working with kids, that's…really great. Admirable."

Joss appreciated the sentiment coming from someone who did what he did. "The kids make it fun," she said as her cell beeped a third time. She picked up the phone and gave Brady a sheepish smile. "Sorry. Let me reassure my friend you're not a serial killer."

He chuckled. "What time did you give her before she should call the police?"

Heat flooded her cheeks. "Well, now, if I told you that, then you'd know how long to wait until you could stuff me in the back of your nondescript van."

Smiling, he nodded. "Right."

She opened Christina's messages.

The first one read: *Woman! I need deets!*

Then: *Ooh, Brady's a good name.*

Finally: *Be safe. Use a condom. And don't forget to call me!!! Also, DEETS!!!*

Joss shook her head. In so many ways, she and Christina Flores were total opposites, but they just clicked. She wrote back, *TY! Will do!*, then set the phone to vibrate and dropped it to the blanket.

When she lifted her gaze, Brady was watching her. "In all seriousness, I'm glad you did that. But, in case it needs to be said, I'm not a serial killer."

She couldn't help her smile. "Good to know. Neither am I."

"You had me worried," he said, giving her a wink.

"It's always the quiet ones."

"Are you quiet, Joss?"

BOOM!

Joss flinched into his side, her heart racing. She'd been so deep into Brady's scorching gaze that the explosion of the first firework caught her off guard.

He leaned into her and chuckled. "Jumpy?"

"No," she said, leaning into him so he could hear her over the constant thunder of the colorful firework display. "Just didn't realize they were starting already."

He nodded and turned his gaze to the show. But though her surprise faded, her heart rate never returned to normal. And it had nothing to do with the red, white, and blue starbursts lighting up the sky. A mere inch separated her body from Brady's, and despite the loud splendor of the fireworks, he dominated her senses. The heat from his arm warmed hers, and made her long for the real heat skin-on-skin contact would bring. Sitting so close, that clean scent she'd noticed earlier, like soap and sun and male, was all she could smell now, and she wondered how much more potent it would be if she pressed her nose, her lips, to his throat, his jaw, his mouth and breathed it in from the source.

Even as Brady sat watching something as simple as fireworks, he didn't seem to relax. Tension clung to the hard set of his jaw, the tight bunching of his shoulders. He was a big man. Obviously strong, apparently deadly, given his profession. She couldn't decide if his intensity thrilled her, or scared her just a little. Maybe both.

He glanced over and caught her looking. Joss dropped her gaze and hoped the cover of night hid the heat blooming on her face. When she peeked from under her lashes, he was still watching her.

Her stomach flopped and her hand fisted the soft cotton of the blanket. A tingle ran through her center that made her catch her breath against the sudden urge to push him back, crawl on top of him, and kiss him until all that tension melted out of his body. Right here. Right now. No matter the spectators, or the fact he was nearly a stranger.

A very hot, damn sexy, purportedly non-serial-killer stranger.

She saw her own desire mirrored back at her. Brady's mouth dropped open and his dark eyes narrowed and blazed in the night.

It took everything she had to return her attention to the fireworks. Or at least pretend to. Because her body jangled with awareness of his until her muscles ached from the strain of holding herself in place. *This is crazy*. Maybe. Probably. But the dampness between her legs wasn't the result of the early September heat.

His breath ghosted over her ear, erupting ticklish chills on her neck and arms. "I'm going to kiss you here, Joss." The tip of his finger skimmed her cheek.

Heart in her throat, she nodded.

Brady pressed a lingering kiss to her cheekbone. Her hands fisted as she struggled not to turn her head and offer her lips. She was already throwing her no-touching admonition out the window.

"Here," he said, touching her jaw.

She nodded and his lips dragged along the line of her jaw.

"Here, too." His finger pressed against the soft spot right

in front of her ear.

She tilted her head and gave him more space to nuzzle her. Surely he could hear her heartbeat over the fireworks, because she could feel her pulse pound under every inch of her skin.

What the hell was she doing? She should really put a stop to this.

He drew an imaginary line beginning at the indent behind her ear and running down her neck. She nodded without him even asking the question. He chuckled in her ear but then his lips were kissing with the lightest suction down her neck.

Applause erupted around them. Joss snapped out of her haze of lust. Brady pulled back and gave her a look that promised a whole helluva lot more where that came from.

Holy crap. She'd never survive it.

Suddenly, the field was in motion, people packing up their belongings and beelining for their cars. Soon, Old Town would be a gridlocked mess. No use fighting it.

He rose and held out a hand to help her up. She accepted, the surrounding heat of his grip reigniting the trembling need inside her. "Thank you," she said.

He didn't let go. "Did you enjoy it?"

She gaped up at him.

Brady's dark eyes filled with humor and he nodded toward the river. "The fireworks."

She nailed him with a you're-so-full-of-shit-even-though-you're-crazy-hot glare. Or, at least, that's what she was thinking. "Yeah. Fireworks were great. Were they good for you?"

"Spectacular." He guided Joss to the side, then bent to lift and fold her blanket.

"Here. I'll do that." She accepted it from him and quickly reduced the cotton to a thick square.

"Don't forget your book." He retrieved it from the grass, then stopped and angled it at the nearest streetlight. His eyebrows flew up as he turned the cover toward her and pointed. "SEALs?" He sighed and shook his head, affecting a long-suffering expression. He tapped his fingers against the picture. "You know, it's really hard work posing for all these covers."

She yanked it from his hands, then whacked him in the stomach with it. "Shut up." Geez. His stomach was like a brick wall, solid and unmoving. She wondered if all of him was that hard.

"I'm just saying," he said with a chuckle, then grabbed the pizza box, untouched sandwich, and last bag of chips.

"Uh-huh. Pain in the ass." *Bet his ass is hard, too.*

He nodded. "So, uh. Where are you parked?"

Joss pointed across the field. "Lot behind that building over there."

He held out a hand, indicating she should go ahead. "I'll walk you."

She thought about protesting, but honestly she wasn't ready to have them part. What exactly *was* she ready for? She didn't know that either.

But would it really be so wrong to indulge a little? Or even a lot? After the day she had, it might be just what the soldier, er, doctor ordered. She ignored the little voice that whispered she was setting herself up to get hurt. As usual.

They moved into the streaming sea of people. The breeze made the thin cotton of her wrap skirt float around her legs and emphasized just how damp her thong was. Despite the crowd, she was struck by how dominating Brady's presence was beside her. She wasn't short, but she almost felt it next to him. And whenever approaching walkers necessitated that they proceed single file instead of side by side, he'd place his hand on the small of her back and guide her in front of him. The gesture revealed a man with impressively good manners, but the touch made her muscles jump and her body yearn for more every time.

"Oh, hold up. Can we go this way for a second?" He nodded toward the river.

"Uh, sure. Why?"

He shrugged and looked away. "I just really hate to waste food."

She nodded, still not sure what he had in mind, and when he held out his hand, she grabbed it. That big, calloused grip around hers made her willing to follow his lead. Again.

Crossing the grass, they approached an old, shabbily dressed man seated under a streetlamp on a bench at the park's edge, a beat-up duffel bag at his feet, and a small, scruffy dog curled beside him. She hadn't seen him over the heads of the other people, but apparently Brady had. Realization flooded Joss and her heart tripped over itself.

"Hey, man. Can I pet your dog?" Brady asked.

The homeless man grinned and nodded. "You betcha. Just move real slow-like. He's an attack dog in disguise."

The dog was old as dirt and, if he'd ever been an attack dog, was long in retirement. He lifted two sagging eyelids and stretched out. Brady released her hand, then crouched down and stroked the mutt's wiry fur. "Looks like I caught him at a good time."

"Yeah," the man said, eyeing the dog with the kind of

affection reserved for a best friend. "You a soldier, son?"

With a nod, Brady said, "Army Special Forces."

Whoa. That was news to Joss. Not just any old soldier, then.

"That right? I was a grunt back in the day. 'Nam."

"Jungle's no better than the sandbox, I suspect." Brady reached out a hand. "Brady Scott."

Her heart thundered against her breastbone. She'd thought Brady all intense playfulness, but with his kindness and respect to this homeless man he'd just proved himself more compassionate than most. Given how she'd grown up, she'd always been a sucker for a compassionate soul.

"You got that right." The effort it took for the man to extend his arm and return the handshake was obvious, but the gleam in his eyes said he didn't mind making it. "Mike McAffey."

"Nice to meet you." Brady looked up at the departing crowds. "Well, I guess we best be heading home." He stood. "Oh, hey. I've got half a pizza and an untouched sandwich here. Any chance you might like them? Sure would save me from carrying them home."

Just like that, Brady let the man retain his dignity, too. Mike's glance roamed from the items in Brady's hand to the dog to Joss. "If it would help you out, I'm sure me and Goose wouldn't mind."

"Goose?" she asked as Brady settled the food on the bench by the duffel bag.

"You ever seen how mean geese can be?" He nodded at the sleeping dog. "Goose."

She chuckled.

"All right, have a good night, Mike," Brady said with a

wave.

Mike waved back, already unwrapping the sandwich.

Brady grabbed her hand again and led her through the crowd. When they were far enough away from Mike and Goose, she peeked up at him, her chest full of pride. Ridiculous, maybe, since she hardly knew him, but that didn't stop it from being there. "That was really nice."

He shrugged. "No sense letting food go to waste."

"I mean it, Brady. You did a really nice thing." She squeezed his fingers.

He looked down at the grass, his discomfort with her praise palpable between them.

She knocked her shoulder into his arm. "I might just have to stop calling you 'sailor boy' after that."

He peered down at her. "Really?"

She tapped a finger against her lips. "We'll see."

Their need to wind their way through a line of moving cars cut off their conversation, but she could've sworn she heard him mumbling something about his balls getting busted and she couldn't help but chuckle.

They stepped up on the opposite curb and a body crashed into Joss, sending her stumbling. Brady bit out a curse as he caught her and pulled her in against his chest, steadying her. At least, that was his intent. The press of all that hard muscle against the length of her liquefied her insides and melted her knees. She looked up to find a dark scowl on his face at the two teenagers who had run past them. He heaved a breath that was nearly a growl, but his expression eased a little as he met her gaze. "You okay?"

"Yeah, thanks," she said, hearing the breathlessness of her voice but unable to stop it. Maybe she should've been alarmed at the rigid tremble of his muscles and the fierce expression, but all she felt was gratitude for his protectiveness. Given how she grew up, she'd rarely had someone who looked out for her, defended her.

"Come on." Arm around her shoulders, Brady guided them down the sidewalk, all the while keeping her body tucked tight against his. Her brain said to pull away, that she didn't know him well enough to allow him to hold her this way, but she couldn't convince her body to listen. His muscles flexed against her, forcing into her mind's eye the image of what it would feel like to have all that strength and power moving over her, into her.

What was wrong with her? *He's a freaking stranger!* Sorta.

She shivered and felt her nipples press rigid into the soft cups of her bra.

Brady's hand tightened on her shoulder.

"I'm back there," she said as they entered the wide gravel parking lot. "In the corner."

"In the dark spot?" He frowned.

She elbowed him. "Wasn't dark when I parked, sailor boy."

"Mm-hmm." She felt the response rumble from his chest more than she heard it.

Dodging the cars inching toward the exit, she was pleased to see that more than half the cars had already departed the lot. It wouldn't take as long to get out of here as she feared. Finally, they arrived at her old truck, all she'd been able to afford when she'd started her assistant director job at the center a couple of years ago.

"This is yours?"

"Yeah. Surprised?" The tank of a red pickup wasn't much to look at, truth be told, but it got around and hauled a ton, which is why she kept it. Came in handy at work all the time.

He rolled his big shoulders, like he was working out a kink. "With you, always."

She leaned back against the driver's side door as the cars beside them backed out of their spots. "Is that a bad thing?"

Brady stepped in front of her and pulled the blanket, book, phone, and keys from her hands, then set them on the edge of the truck bed. When his gaze returned to hers, his eyes were filled with heat, wide and penetrating and intense. Erotic tension filled the narrow space between them and made it hard to breathe. His tall, broad body surrounded her and blocked out the rest of the world. All she could see was his open lips and blazing eyes, all she could feel was the quick rise and fall of his chest, and all she knew was the burning desire for *something* to happen.

He leaned in and his tongue flicked his lip, once, twice.

Her arms froze against her sides. Her hands fisted. Joss's equilibrium faltered, leaving her body feeling as if she were boneless and floating. Her insides clenched.

He paused a hair's breadth away from her mouth. His rapid exhales wisped over her lips. "Not a bad thing at all."

She swallowed hard.

Bad idea. Bad idea. Such a bad idea.

"Oh, God, do it," she rasped.

Chapter Three

Brady devoured Joss in a way that was too hard and possessive for a first kiss, but he couldn't stop himself. Aggression still flowed through his blood at the punks who'd nearly knocked her to the ground, and the chemistry between him and this infuriatingly sexy woman was damn near incendiary. If all that wasn't enough, her pleading words had detonated the last of his self-control, assuming he'd ever had any where she was concerned.

He sucked and nipped at her full lips, plowed his hands through her pinned-up hair, and stepped into her body until there was no space between them, until he could feel her puckered nipples press against his chest. Christ, she was soft and warm. He couldn't get enough of those sweet mewling noises working their way up her throat, of her traceable curves squirming against him.

This girl was one damn fine distraction. Just what Brady needed.

Grasping her face, he stroked his tongue against her lips, praying for her to open to his exploration. She did, but not in the way he expected. *She* invaded *him*, her tongue pushing forward to entwine with his.

Oh, damn. She smelled like peaches and tasted like sin. And there was that piercing, hard and pebbled and slick against the softness of his mouth. Brady had thought he couldn't get any harder, but the wet slide of that metal ball shot his body into overdrive. He rocked his hips into hers and groaned in victory when she pressed right back and scratched her fingers against his scalp.

Brady was no stranger to women, but this one was full of contradictions that drove him wild. She had a smart mouth and a sharp wit, but blushed in a way that revealed vulnerability. She gave off an untouchable vibe, but jumped into him at the sound of fireworks. With the tattoos, pink highlights, and tongue piercing, she came off as rebellious, but she worked with kids. Joss was like a puzzle with ever-changing pieces, and it threw him off-kilter, made him feel like he was on a collision course he couldn't avoid and wouldn't want to anyway. The desperate noises she made, the enthusiastic sway and press of her curves, her futile effort to grasp and tug at his short hair—he'd remember the sound and feel of her for a long time.

She was marking him, as surely as the metal that pierced her tongue and the ink that tattooed her skin marked her.

At the thought, unease flashed through him. There was nothing permanent about what was going on here. And there never would be. He groaned against her skin. *For fuck's sake, throw yourself a pity party later, Scott.* He focused on the fact that she was as game as he was to give in to the crazy attraction between them. Icing on his lust cake. *That's* what this was about.

Memories like these were good, necessary, because they were all he'd ever let himself have.

He shifted, bringing his leg between hers. Joss whimpered into their kiss as his thigh pressed in tight right where she was eager to have him, judging by the way she ground herself forward against his quad. Damn it all but the heat pouring through that thin skirt was fantastic and infuriating, because he knew it wouldn't compare to the searing grip of being buried deep inside her.

Needing more of her, he tilted her face back and dragged his lips along the line of her jaw. Remembering how she'd shivered on the blanket, he paused at her ear, nipping and licking, all the while reveling in the rasping breaths she released and the guiding hand she kept on the back of his head.

"Oh, God. What are we—"

"Nothing you don't want," he whispered into her ear. "You just say the word and I back off." Even if it would leave him unable to walk.

She rocked her hips into him, creating a maddening friction that made his blood pound through his veins. Continuing on his journey, Brady dragged his tongue down her neck, relishing the salty-sweet taste of her skin. His hands joined in the exploration, cupping the sides of her breasts.

She threw her head back on a gasping moan.

Watching her face closely, he swiped his thumbs over her raised nipples, clearly outlined by her thin shirt.

Joss's whole body sagged against the door of her truck and her mouth dropped into an erotic oval. Damn, she looked fucking gorgeous against the chrome and glass and faded red steel of the old Ford.

Glancing to his right, Brady surveyed the wide, emptying parking lot. They were alone in this corner now, and the only remaining line of cars snaked closer to the far side, along the street.

God, he really wanted her. He had no idea what she was game for, but he wanted to be so far inside her, all the shit in his head would go away for good. He could just lift her up, work his way under that flimsy skirt, and take her against the truck. It would be so easy. Not that he would actually do that to her. But damn if the urges weren't kicking him in the ass.

Shoving the tangled thoughts away, he found her neck with his lips again. The little gasp she gave echoed through his body until he was strung tight and aching. *Goddammit.* When was the last time a woman had thrown his body into this much of a frenzy?

Her hands gripped onto his shoulders. "Brady."

The low, throaty sound of her voice filled him with satisfaction as he continued to taste her.

"Sailor boy," she said louder.

He drew back, a retort on the tip of his tongue. He'd make good on his promise to cure her of saying that yet.

"Your place or mine?"

The question froze the words in his mouth and his brain went blank even as his cock strained against his shorts. He blinked and narrowed his gaze, and slid his thumb to rest over the staccato beat of the artery in her neck, assessing her every way he could. "You sure?"

She gave him a wicked grin, though its impact was lessened by her breathlessness. "One-night-only offer. Going, going—"

"Yours."

She nodded to her truck and gave him a little push. "Get in."

Brady hauled ass around to the passenger side. He'd pick his truck up at the end of his run tomorrow. She unlocked the door just as he reached for the handle. *One night only*. This woman was freaking perfect for him. And exactly what he needed right now.

He slid up onto the wide bench seat of the big beast of a truck and pulled the creaky door closed behind him. She fumbled getting the keys into the ignition for a moment, but then the engine came to life on a low rumble. He clicked his seat belt into place, his brain a racing train of mental high fives and erotic plans to show Joss his appreciation for taking him home.

The engine went dead.

His gaze cut to Joss, who sat staring straight ahead, her hand on the key.

"Are you o— Whoa. What—"

Joss shot across the seat at Brady and crawled into his lap, straddling him and grasping for his face. Then she kissed him, lips pulling, tongue probing, hips grinding down against a pronounced bulge.

She never did this. *Never*. But did she ever need it. And why not? She was single. She was an adult. And, dammit, she wanted him.

Maybe it was seeing Ethan this morning. Or maybe it was the wound Ethan's new pregnant fiancée reopened. Or maybe it was no more complicated than *this* man making her want and feel things she'd never felt before. And it didn't hurt that he wanted her—that was apparent in the urgency of his grip and the rigid hard-on between her legs. She needed that feeling of being wanted, even if it was fleeting, temporary, just for this one night.

All she knew was she couldn't wait to have him. Didn't want to.

Brady's hands stroked over her breasts and she gasped, and then his fingers found the hem of her shirt, her bare stomach.

A red-hot thrill spiraled through her at the skin-on-skin contact, following by a quick niggling thought: *You're doing this here because you're afraid you'll get cold feet before you get home. Or he will.*

She shoved the thought away and gave in to the heat of his hands palming her breasts over her bra. She spared a glance at the window over his shoulder and found the lot had emptied save for a dark car parked here or there. Though they were in public, they were alone here, sheltered by the dark shadow the building threw.

Brady's hands withdrew and he grasped hers. "Are you sure about this? I don't want—"

"Is this too crazy?" Doubt and an old insecurity squeezed her stomach. *Want me.*

He stroked his knuckles over her cheek. "Only in a good way. I just don't want you doing something you'll regret."

She shrugged, forcing a casualness she didn't really feel. "I wouldn't regret you, Brady."

He tilted his head, appraising her. Something dark passed over his expression, but then Joss squirmed, reminding them both just how close they were. His hands gripped her hips and stilled her movement. "Sweetness, I've got only the loosest grip on myself right now."

Her stomach eased and the nickname further warmed her skin. "Then why are we still talking?" When the concern faded from his gaze and he smiled, she unhooked his seat belt and grabbed for his shirt. "Show me what you have under here, sailor boy."

His eyes narrowed and filled with hot intent, but he reached over his shoulder and tugged the gray tee off in that sexy one-handed way guys did. Before she could get on with the ogling, he'd grabbed her, kissed the slope of skin where neck turned to shoulder, and then bit her. Not hard enough to hurt, but hard enough to know exactly what he'd done.

She gasped, not from pain, but surprise.

With a possessive grip of his hand, he soothed his thumb over the spot and threw her a cocky smile. "I'll cure you of that nickname one way or the other."

No way she was giving up that taunt. His reactions were too freaking priceless. "You're still talking," she said breathlessly, dropping her gaze to appreciate the cut ridges of muscle covering his abdomen. If he'd intended the bite as punishment, that wasn't how her body perceived it if the dampness between her legs was any indication. Her hands gave in to the need to see if all that muscle was as hard as it looked. *Yup. Geez.*

He crushed his lips to hers. His tongue filled her mouth, plunging, swirling, simulating the movement she yearned to feel elsewhere. "Take your hair down," he rasped, then dove back into the kiss, stealing her breath, commanding she submit to his desire. Taking orders wasn't her usual MO, but for him, for this, she'd make an exception. With clumsy fingers she removed the pins and band, dropped them…somewhere. Her hair cascaded around her shoulders.

"Fuck, yeah," he whispered, his hands gripping the thick strands of hair and forcing her to move how he wanted her to move, stay where he wanted her to stay.

She reached for her shirt and pulled, forcing them to break the kiss. Brady released her hair and grasped her arms before she could remove the cotton completely. "Lean back." Bracing a hand on the dashboard behind her, Joss obeyed, Brady's body following. Shirt still raised, his tongue found the line of her bra, traced from one side of her chest to the other, slowly, teasingly, *maddeningly*. She was trembling now, from the adrenaline of this crazy moment, from the sheer force of her arousal.

"What is this?" he asked, caressing the tattoo covering her heart.

"It's a sparrow," she whispered. It had been her first.

"Wish I could see it better."

Another time. She'd barely restrained herself from saying the words. They wouldn't have been true anyway, right?

The calloused pads of his fingers played at one bra cup's edge. He glanced up at her, eyes on fire. She nodded.

He pulled the satiny fabric down, exposing her heated flesh to the hot nighttime air. "Perfect," he murmured against her skin. Kissing and licking around the curves of her breast, he circled her nipple until she thought she might beg him to touch her there. And then he was. Kissing. Flicking. Sucking deep into his mouth. She arched into it and grabbed on hard to the lean muscle of his shoulder.

Crazy, crazy, totally freaking crazy…oh, so damn good.

Brady tugged the other cup out of the way and treated her right breast to the same worshipful attention...

What was it she'd been thinking again?

His tongue demanded she not waste another brain cell trying to remember.

But then he returned the satin cups to cover her. Joss gasped as the form-fitting material pressed against the rigid peaks of her nipples. "What—"

"Shh." He kissed the corner of her mouth as he settled her shirt into place. "Dammit, Joss, I want to spread you out and explore you all night long. But what I don't want is for anyone to see you exposed. So, shirt on. Okay?"

Warm pressure filled her chest. There was his protectiveness again. For her. "Okay," she whispered. She cupped his face, and that pressure expanded when he softly leaned into her right hand. Like she was a sculptor memorizing his form, she slid her hands down his neck to his shoulders. Sheer power thrummed under all that male skin.

She should be scared of him. Of this. Of what they were doing, in her truck of all places. But her brain paraded his treatment of Mike, his protectiveness when the teens knocked into her, his support of her texting Christina, and his insistence about her shirt through her mind's eye, and she just let go, gave in, gave herself permission to have this.

Her hands traced the chain of his dog tags and skimmed down the taut pads of his pectorals to his stomach. His muscles flinched under the light, teasing touch, and she smiled. Her fingers trailed into the line of brown hair that ran toward his navel and his mouth dropped open. She swirled a design on his skin that made his breath catch. What she wouldn't do to hear that needful sound from him again and again. Reaching his waistband, she glanced to Brady's intense, dark eyes, much as he had looked to her before.

"Only if you're sure."

She tugged the top button through the hole and drew the zipper down, exposing a pair of black cotton boxers made tight by his straining hard-on.

Breathing faster, shallow, he reached into his rear pocket and tossed his wallet to the seat, then he helped her shove his shorts and boxers down enough to release his cock to her gaze. A streetlight down the row of cars threw just enough diffuse light into the truck's cab that her mouth watered and she swallowed, hard. God, he was thick and veined, swollen with need. She grasped him and his hips jerked upward.

He wrapped a big hand around hers where she held him, stroked him. "Joss. Damn it all…" Her thumb swiped over his head and spread around the slickness. He groaned and grabbed at the length of her skirt again and again until he found the bottom edge and could push it up her thigh.

The heated cab of her truck smelled of the summer night, the cool spice of Brady's aftershave, and the promise of damn hot sex.

When he'd exposed her to the waist, he dragged a finger over the triangle of white silk covering her, then turned his wrist and pressed three fingers between her legs. He stilled when she gasped, his eyes tracking her reaction before he rubbed the sensitive covered skin at the juncture of her thighs.

The press of his fingers made it all the more clear just how wet she was. She moaned at the wild sensations ricocheting through her. Her heartbeat echoed thunderously in the enclosed space of the cab, or maybe that was just her blood pounding against her eardrums. Brady grabbed her hip and stroked her harder, the wet slide of her thong adding an incredible friction. For a long moment, she lost the ability to do anything but feel him touching her, but then she realized her hand had stilled, and no way did she want to be the only one this out of control. She fisted her grip up the length of his thick erection, her thumb swiping over the head before lowering again.

"*Fuck*," he groaned. His hands fell away.

She forced her eyes to focus in the dimness and watched as he fished a condom from his wallet. She arched an eyebrow as he tossed the leather to the side and removed the rubber.

"What?" he asked, his cocky expression both infuriating and sexy as all hell. "I didn't expect anything, I promise. Just had, you know, an avid hope."

She shook her head, but truly she couldn't even work up any fake indignation. Had he not brought the condom, she might be tempted to do something *really* crazy. She was that aroused. Way, way past the point of resisting what her body was demanding she have. *Now*.

Brady placed the latex over his cock, holding himself as he rolled it down to the base. Joss couldn't pull her gaze away. The sight made her stomach flip and the muscles in her core clench.

"Come here, sweetness."

She pushed onto her knees and scooted closer.

He braced a hand against her stomach and met her gaze. "How much do you like these?"

"What?" Dazed, she glanced down.

He rent the flimsy fabric of her thong apart, and a second yank removed the material between her legs altogether. "If they were your favorites, I'll buy you another."

A nervous giggle worked its way up her throat. "You just tore off my thong."

He grinned and tugged her hips over him. She gripped his shoulder with one hand and held her skirt out of the way with the other. Then he was right there, his swollen head poised just below the aching flesh of her center.

She sank down.

"Oh, fuck me," he groaned.

"That's the plan," she managed, her throat tight around the incredible pleasure grasping every part of her. When she had taken him in all the way, Joss paused and let her body adjust to the pressure of his presence inside her. He was a damn big boy.

"You okay?" he rasped.

She nodded and gripped harder onto his shoulder, damp with a thin sheen of sweat. "More than." She began to move, slowly, setting a dragging, teasing pace that had them both panting.

He clutched her hips, anchoring and guiding her. "Too damn hot not to see this," he said, his eyes trained where his body disappeared inside hers.

She curled her hand around the back of Brady's neck and held on. Her center throbbed at his invasion, her thighs strained to keep up the pace, to quicken it, her clit urged her forward, until her body rubbed against his with every stroke.

He slid down in the seat, then grasped her left hand and guided it to the hand strap hanging above the door. "Hold yourself up a little," he said.

She obeyed and held her skirt out of the way as Brady used his massive thighs to hammer his hips upward, fucking her even though she was on top. She moaned long and low and gripped the old leather so hard it bit into her palm. His pace was fast. Hard. Insistent. And gave her body a massive shove toward the explosive free fall that had her name written all over it.

His hand slid off her hip and moved to her mound. He worried his thumb over her clit and Joss threw her head back and swallowed the scream that threatened.

"No, no. Look at me. I want to see you when you come."

Somehow, she found the muscle control to respond. Arousal made the hard angle of his jaw and strong brow stand out. "Oh, God."

"Yeah? I like that one better than 'sailor boy.'"

She nodded.

He pulled his thumb away and she gasped. "Tell me I'm not a sailor."

Her brain swam through her arousal. "What?"

"I want to hear you say it," he said on a harder thrust.

"Seriously?" she gasped.

He arched a brow and gave her maybe the sexiest grin she'd ever seen. His thumb flicked against her clit for a half dozen strokes, then pulled away. "Say it."

She sighed, but it came out sounding like a soft moan. "You're not a sailor," she said, her indignation lost in the softness of her voice.

"That's right." He grinned, returning his thumb to her clit with renewed enthusiasm and luring her toward the edge of her body's pleasure threshold. "You feel so good, Joss. I can forget the whole fucking world when I'm inside you."

What his thumb didn't do, his words finished. Her belly went tight, tight, tighter until he was groaning and she was coming, her muscles pulsing hard around his thrusting cock.

"Oh, sweetness," he whispered, his voice a rough scrape. His shaft erupted inside her, over and over. With two hands, he slammed her down, held her for a long moment, lifted her up and repeated that motion, once, twice, until finally, their bodies stilled.

Joss released the hand strap, and Brady cradled her body against him. Her head fell to his damp shoulder and he stroked her hair off the side of her face. It was a moment more quietly intimate, with him still inside her and his arms around her, than any other she could recall. Just then, she would've sworn she'd known him for years.

He kissed her forehead.

A tight sting settled behind her eyes.

Hell, no! Do not cry on the sex god Special Forces soldier after he just gave you the orgasm of your life.

She blinked the sensation away and forced on her mental big-girl panties. Which brought to mind that she didn't have any to wear now.

"Wow," Brady whispered into the stillness.

"Yeah," she said. What was that aching pressure inside her chest? Out of nowhere, the image of Ethan and his fiancée slammed into her mind's eye so hard she nearly gasped. Why was she thinking of him now?

He kissed her again and squeezed her in the tight circle of his arms. After a long moment, he released her. The suddenly cooler air made her shiver. "Here, let me…" He reached between them and eased her off his lap. "Aw, damn."

"What?" she asked as she straightened her skirt and settled on the big bench seat beside him. She wiped a bead of sweat from her forehead.

"Nothing. Almost slipped off. But I got it." He tied a knot in the condom.

Joss handed him a tissue from the box on the floor. "I'm on the pill, anyway," she whispered.

He nodded and wrapped the condom in the tissue, then hiked up his shorts. When he was all put back together, he looked at her so long she started to squirm. She didn't understand the pensive expression on his face as he stroked his knuckles over her cheek. "I like your hair down."

"Oh? Thanks." She smoothed a hand over her hair, loving how easily, how freely, he gave out these little compliments and considerations. She could so easily imagine herself falling into him. Asking him to come home with her. Making him breakfast. Spending the day with him. Many days. And that scared her.

"Penny for your thoughts?" he asked.

Joss didn't realize how long she'd just been sitting there. She drew her knees up next to her. "I've never done this before."

His eyes went wide. "Had sex?"

"Oh, my God! No! I'm twenty-eight years old. I've had sex before."

Brady held his hands up. "Okay, okay." He blew out a breath. "I just didn't realize what you were—"

She smacked him in the arm. "Such a pain in the ass."

Chuckling, he said, "That's not the tune you were singing a few minutes ago."

Heat bloomed across her face and she waved a hand. "Yeah, well… No, I mean sex in my truck. Sex with a man I've just met. Sex in a freaking parking lot."

He grinned. "That's a lot of firsts."

"I know, right?"

"Well, thank you for sharing them with me." He grasped her hand and squeezed. "Seriously, I had a great time with you tonight. And not just this." He waved to indicate her truck and what had happened there. "The whole night. Dinner. The fireworks."

"Me, too." She wasn't sure what was supposed to happen now. A big old part of her still wanted to make those plans with him. But she knew that wasn't what this was about, and she knew herself well enough to know he made her heart duck and run for cover. She had no doubt he was a good guy, but he was also a player. And he was a soldier who'd move on to his next assignment in a year or two. Neither was going to do anything good for her fear of being left behind.

Cart before horse, much?

Probably. Definitely. She sighed.

One-night-only offer. That's what she'd said. And what a one time it was. She'd never forget this night. As good memories went, it was right up there.

"So, where are you parked? Can I drive you to your car?"

He pulled her hand to his mouth and kissed her knuckles. "Nah. It's only a couple blocks. I'll enjoy the walk."

"Okay." *This is weird*, her mind yelled. *You two are great together. Ask for his number.* She wanted to. She really did. But she couldn't read him. Wasn't sure what he would want. Or what she could risk.

And it wasn't like he was asking for hers.

He gave her a long look full of that intensity she now associated with him. "See you around, Joss."

She nodded and watched him push out of her truck. The door slammed behind him. He stood there, waiting for her to go.

Her stomach clenched as she fastened her seat belt, started the truck, and backed out of her spot. That damn stinging returned at the back of her eyes. She blinked as she pulled up next to him and rolled down the window.

Ask for my number, she thought as she forced herself to smile at him.

He leaned his head through the opening and gave her a long kiss that tasted like more. "Be careful going home."

"I will. It's not far." Her gaze swept over the quiet lot, hiding her face from his view. She didn't want him to see how much she needed him to want her. "Well, good night, sailor boy."

She pulled away, the outraged expression she saw on his face in the rearview mirror making her smile, just a little.

Chapter Four

Virginia LCK 2176.

Without meaning to, Brady committed the truck's license plate number to memory.

It wasn't like he needed that information. Not unless he planned to… No.

This was a one-night-only deal. Exactly his style. He didn't do sleepovers. He didn't call the next day. He didn't make plans. Good as the night had been—and it had been fantastic—he didn't *want* to see Joss again. Something about her made too many "maybes" and "what ifs" float through his brain. Damn if he didn't feel…*good* around her. That kind of connection had a better than average chance of leading down a path he had no intentions of running. Ever.

Fuckin' A.

Brady crossed the lot and tried to ignore just how much Joss still dominated his senses. His mouth remembered the cool metal of her piercing. Rubbing his thumb against his fingers, he could almost feel the moisture of her peaches and cream on his skin. His thighs still carried her warm weight. And his dick was ready to volunteer for round two in the truck sex Olympics.

Out of habit, he made a scan of his surroundings as he walked up Oronoco to Fairfax, where his new Land Rover was parked. He'd treated himself to the wheels when he'd returned stateside back in June. It was pretty much the only thing of value he owned. Buying it was probably stupid since he had no idea what he'd do with it once he was done here, but maybe he'd just give it to his sister Alyssa—her car was such a POS anyway.

The Rover unlocked with a click and a flash of taillights. Brady got in and started the engine.

You should've gotten her number.

Aw, hell no.

He didn't even entertain the argument. He pulled out, drove up Fairfax, and waited at the light, his brain on autopilot. To block out the thoughts slinking around the edge of his consciousness looking for a weak spot, he cranked up the tunes and allowed the persistent bass beat to drive the bullshit away.

Twenty minutes later, he parked in front of his new town house. Well, it wasn't really his, since he was renting, and it wasn't new, since the whole community was at least seventy years old, but it's where he'd be laying his head for the next eighteen to twenty-four months. Having an actual address where he could receive mail and get pizzas delivered was him being more settled than he'd been in a long time. Maybe ever. And damn if that didn't make him as restless as a short-timer awaiting orders.

His place was second from the end on the left side of a horseshoe-shaped grouping of brick town houses. Fairlington had been built at the beginning of World War II to house the office workers at the then-brand-new Pentagon, so it was kinda appropriate he was living here now. He slid the key in the lock and stepped inside, doing a sweep over the dark, still parking lot before securing the door behind him.

Home empty home.

Uniforms, workout gear, a handful of civvies, and a few boxes of necessities were about all he owned at this point, aside from the bed he'd had delivered the previous night. He'd reported for duty at Army Staff, Pentagon, right after the Fourth of July, and had crashed at an acquaintance's apartment while he searched for a place. Guess he'd have to pick up a few things to fill the house soon. No rush, though. The idea of acquiring a bunch of possessions felt as constraining as humping a fifty-pound ruck over twenty miles of rough terrain.

Actually, he'd feel more at home on a ruck march.

Brady made his way through the dark first floor to check the locks on the back door, the only sound in the place the restless jingle of the keys in his hand. He glanced out back at his small fenced-in patio. All secure. He grabbed a beer from the fridge—the case a housewarming gift from the work buddies who helped him move in—and made his way upstairs. He stopped to use the head and debated showering, but he wasn't ready to wash away Joss's scent yet. Couldn't he allow himself that much?

In his bedroom, the overhead light was harsh against the bare white walls and closed plastic blinds. He dug through one, two, three boxes before he found the new sheets he'd bought. Oh, hey, there was the new shower curtain, too. The Target home department might as well have exploded in his room.

He ripped the plastic wrapping off the dark gray sheets and unfolded them. Square pieces of cardboard fell out as he did. Damn if these sheets weren't stiff as shit. And he thought army-issue was bad. Maybe he was supposed to wash them first? He shrugged and whipped the fitted sheet out over the new queen mattress. S'all good.

After he got the sheets on, he opened the new pillows and wrestled the fucking things into the pillowcases. That was some bullshit right there. But, whatever.

Finally, he unzipped the bag encasing his new comforter and spread that out, gray pinstripes running lengthwise on the otherwise black blanket.

He grabbed his beer and took a long swig as he admired his handiwork. Look at him being all domestic.

He sat heavily on the edge of the bed and kicked off his sneakers. He yanked a box closer to the bed's edge and placed his watch on it, then ditched his tee and shorts and crossed the room to kill the light. In bed, he stared up at the dark ceiling and all he could hear was the *nothingness*. Holy hell, it was quiet. No night noises. No quiet conversations. No teammates snoring. *Dammit*. He wasn't used to being this alone with himself.

He got out of bed. At the window, he yanked up a blind and opened a window. He could just make out the noise of traffic on King Street. Somewhere close, a dog barked. Every once in a while, the wind murmured through the big tree on the other side of the courtyard. Yeah, that was better.

Horizontal again, Brady locked down wandering thoughts

of his one-night stand and gave in to the lure of sleep. Between the drinking, the late night, and the mind-numbing orgasm, he could use some serious shut-eye right about now.

What felt like ten seconds passed.

Bang, bang, bang.

His eyes flicked open and squinted against the light that was soft enough he knew it was still early.

Bang, bang, bang, bang, bang.

"What in the fuck?" He pushed into a sitting position and glared at the wall behind his head. Whoever was banging was also playing music.

What time is it?

He made a grab for the watch and gawked. 6:52 a.m. A big bucket of pissed off parked itself in his chest. Unfucking-acceptable.

Out of bed, he hauled on his shorts and grabbed a shirt.

Bang, bang, thud.

He had to nip this shit right in the bud. Annoyance flared as each new *bang* prodded at his anger like a mean dog being poked with a sharp stick. And with him, it didn't take much poking. Quick-to-anger seemed to be hardwired into him.

Down the stairs. Out the front door. Across the ten feet of sidewalk to the small stoop on the end unit next door. And then he did some banging of his own. On his neighbor's front door.

Hands on his hips, Brady waited. For a moment, he hung his head and heaved a deep breath. No sense taking the guy's head off. First impressions and all that.

A fumbling at the door caught his attention, and then it opened just enough for a face to peek through the gap.

What in the hell?

Joss whipped the door open and blinked. Twice. *Holy crap!* "Sailor boy?"

"What— Joss?" He glared at her.

"What are you—" they began at the same time.

"Wait. Do you live here?" Brady asked, scrubbing his hand over his hair.

"Uh, yeah. Last time I checked. How did you…" Ice flushed through her system. "Did you…follow me?"

His mouth dropped open. "What? No. I live here."

Oh, no. I had crazy sex with a crazy man. She grabbed the doorknob and pulled it closer, ready to slam it if he made any sudden moves. "Listen. I'm very sorry, Brady. But this is my house," she said, making full use of the calm but firm teacher-like voice she sometimes had to use with her kids.

His brow cranked down and the glare returned. After a moment, his eyes went wide right before he rolled them. "Right. And I live *there*." He pointed next door. "Which is why I'm *here* now. What in the name of all that's holy are you banging on before seven o'clock on a Sunday morning, woman?"

She felt her mouth open, but her brain was too busy playing catch-up to respond. "Wait." She pushed out her screen door and stepped onto the cool bricks of her stoop. The FOR RENT sign was gone from the garden of the unit next to hers. "Are you telling me—"

"That we're neighbors? Apparently, that's an affirmative."

"That is…" Joss didn't even have the word. Could it be…

oh, let's see…*crazy*? She cupped her hands to her cheeks, looked at his expectant and equally bewildered face, and burst out laughing. She tried to rein it in, but there was no stopping the laughter. She was neighbors with her never-see-him-again one-night stand! She clapped a hand over her mouth and fell back against the wall next to her door. The snorting should've embarrassed her, but it only spurred on the hilarity until her eyes filled with tears that crept out the corners of her eyes and streamed down her face.

Brady's gaze narrowed. The more annoyed he got, the more she couldn't stop. And dang if he wasn't just as sexy at seven in the morning as he'd been in the dark of the night. Even wearing his mad face.

He arched a brow. "You done yet?"

She held up a finger, asking him to hold on the only way she could. Finally, she could speak again. "Oh, come on. You have to admit it's a little funny." She pressed her lips together and schooled her expression.

He rolled his eyes again. "Yeah, yeah. Let it out already."

She shook her head and fought the tremendous pressure to laugh again. She tried to distract herself by getting in a good ogle of her one-night-stand-sex-god-soldier-new-neighbor, but then she realized he was wearing the same gray tee and khaki cargo shorts as last night, and she lost it again. It was like he'd done the walk of shame, without the walk…

Through the humor, a thought crept in. *And what are you wear—* Joss gasped and slapped her arms across her chest. "Holy shit, I don't have a bra on."

Of course, her comment drew Brady's gaze to her chest, which he couldn't see only because of her arms. But was there *any* possible chance he hadn't seen her boobs through this thin white tank? The brevity of her boxer shorts was becoming more and more noticeable, too.

He smirked. "You've been standing there giving me shit for like two minutes, and you just *now* remembered how you're dressed?"

Heat bloomed across Joss's cheeks.

He waved at her body, his eyes lingering above her arms until she followed his gaze. The sparrow's wing was visible above the neckline of her tank. "Your little getup there has been the only redeeming feature to my morning so far."

She huffed. "You mean, besides learning you'll have the pleasure of my company as your neighbor?"

And there was the reappearance of that blazing dark gaze. "Will I, now?"

"Oh, my God. I didn't mean it like *that*." *Although…* No. *Nonono.* "You really do excel at pain in the ass, don't you?"

Brady shrugged, all traces of his earlier annoyance gone. "So, seriously though, what *were* you doing?"

"Oh. I'm sorry. I didn't realize anyone had moved in. When did you, anyway?"

"Friday night. And 'moving in' is a relative term since I own almost nothing yet."

"Well, that explains it. I was at the center late on Friday. Anyway…I was trying to put together a really freaking annoying bookcase. If it makes it up to you any, I smashed my fingers at least three times." She held up her hand to show him the discoloration forming under her thumbnail.

He grimaced. "Damn. That's gonna leave a mark. Well, I could help you later, if you want. You know, after you go put a bra on. Though, don't do it on my account."

Her hand whipped out and smacked his chest. "Shut up."

He leaned in and whispered, "You know, it's entirely possible I've already seen your breasts."

Joss scoffed, her nipples perking up at the reminder. She crossed her arms again. "Yeah, but that was different."

His expression was all skepticism. "I can't wait to hear this."

"Well, just, that was, you know, during…"

He waved a hand and urged her to continue. "During…"

"*You know*. You're totally ruining the good-guy-vibe you had going on a minute ago there with your offer of help."

"Sweetness, don't ever confuse me with a good guy."

Something in her gut didn't like that he'd said that about himself. All she could picture was the way he'd treated the homeless man. She'd always believed you could tell a lot about a person's character by how they treated those who could do nothing for them. Given how she'd grown up, she would know. For a moment, she got tangled in things she wanted to say to him, but shouldn't. She shook her head and gave him a small smile.

They stood looking at one another, neither speaking.

"So…," she said.

"Well," he began at the same time.

They chuckled.

A screen door slammed closed across the courtyard, and Brady glanced away. "Where's your truck, anyway?" He nodded at the empty space in front of her house. Each unit had one space in the circular lot inside the courtyard. Now, like their houses, even their assigned parking spaces were side by side.

"Oh. Someone was in my spot when I got home last night.

I wasn't up to knocking on doors about it so I just parked down the street."

Brady nodded. "Ah. Well, sorry I interrupted your construction project." He took a step back.

"I'm the one who should apologize. I really didn't know anyone was over there yet."

He shrugged. "No harm done," he said as he stepped down off her stoop. "Have a good day, Joss."

"You too," she said, hating to see him go, but knowing she'd be seeing a lot more of him. Her stomach fluttered.

"Hey," he called as he reached his porch. "Know any good places for breakfast around here? I don't exactly have food."

"Oh, sure. There are a couple diners close by, and there's a coffee shop and some fast food restaurants in the shopping center up the street." *Don't say it.* "Or—" She glanced down at her feet and wiggled her toes.

"Or?"

She peered through her lashes at him. "Or you could join me for breakfast. Coffee's on. And I'm kinda badass with a waffle maker."

Chapter Five

Brady's instincts were shouting "retreat" while his stomach was all about the homemade waffles. He looked at his door with the word "no" on his lips, but it was just breakfast with his new neighbor, for fuck's sake. *Your very hot new neighbor. Who you slept with last ni—* "You know what? Waffles sound awesome."

She smiled, and Brady grew that much more satisfied with his seat-of-the-pants answer. "Yeah?"

He nodded. "Gimme five and I'll be over."

"Okay." Joss opened her door. "Just let yourself in." She disappeared inside.

He stared at her empty porch for a moment and then went in his house. *What are you doing, Scott?* "I'm having waffles, goddammit." He jogged up the steps and ditched his clothes in a pile in the bathroom. He grabbed the shower curtain package and tore it open, then shook out the dark blue fabric. "Aw, shit," he said. He'd forgotten to buy the curtain rings.

In the tub, he lathered up a bar of soap in his hands before doing a quick scrub over his entire body. He scooped handfuls of water from the faucet to rinse off, then toweled dry, that little voice bitching at him about why a shower was necessary to eat waffles. He brushed his teeth and combed his short hair without meeting his own gaze in the mirror.

After he pulled on a pair of jeans and a clean shirt, he hustled downstairs. As he reached the door, he realized he'd forgotten shoes, but then shrugged and headed to Joss's.

"Knock, knock," he called as he opened her door.

"I'm in here. Come on in," she called from the kitchen. Her place was laid out identical to his, but that's where the similarities ended. Where his house was monochrome, hers was a riot of color. One living room wall and an overstuffed sofa were a deep plum, and two framed autumn landscapes that hung above her couch added greens, oranges, golds, and reds that were echoed in the curtains, pillows, and rug. The warm brown on the other walls continued into the dining room, which had a dark red accent wall and long curtains with an intricate, colorful pattern. Where his house was empty, picture frames, knickknacks, books, and overflowing shelves filled every space here.

She flew into the dining room, cutting off his inspection of her home. "Hey," she said with a smile.

"Hey. Need help?"

"Nope. I'll just set this stuff out and the waffle iron should be ready to go." She laid out the place mats, plates, and utensils next to one another at the small square table, giving Brady time to notice she'd changed clothes, too. Cut-off jean shorts replaced the rolled-up men's boxers she'd been wearing, and the lacy outline of a bra was visible through the white tank. Which was somehow just as sexy. "Coffee?" she asked, waving him into the kitchen with her.

"Please. Black."

"Oh, me too. Hope you don't mind it strong."

"No such thing as strong coffee in my book."

"That's the truth," she said as she poured him a big mug full. "Here you go."

He took a long sip, his gaze dragging over her long, wavy brown hair, pink strands mixed in. She'd had it up in a sloppy bun when he'd arrived earlier. Had she let it down for him? The thought shouldn't please him the way it did. "Good coffee. Thanks."

She smiled. "Okay, you want to go classic and have them plain? Or I can put chocolate chips or blueberries in them. Or a combination."

Brady surveyed the ingredients she'd laid out on the small counter. "Some of each?"

"You got it." She scooped and poured the batter, clearly comfortable working in the kitchen. And didn't that throw him for a little bit of a loop yet again. A rebellious-looking woman who was at home in the kitchen. He glanced down to the *Courage* tattoo on her foot. Hell, she was even barefoot. The only thing she wasn't was preg— *Don't even go there.*

"How long you lived here?" he asked to change the subject in his own mind.

"Three years," she said as she turned the iron. "I rent, too. Saving up for a house someday, but who knows how long that'll take."

He tipped his cup to her. "That's a great goal."

She opened the iron and removed the first golden-brown

waffle. Its buttery, sweet scent filled the kitchen and had his stomach growling. "Yeah?" She shrugged and busied herself with pouring the batter, this time with chocolate chips mixed in. "What about you?"

"What?"

"Any big goals?"

"Getting promoted to staff sergeant is my goal at the moment."

"Oh, yeah? That's great, Brady. When will you find out?"

Damn good question. Maybe when Dr. Dolittle gives my head a clean bill of health? "Not sure yet."

Joss kept the small talk flowing between them as the plate of waffles stacked up. She was a complete natural at the cooking and the conversation. But the uncertainties Brady'd had about coming over refused to disappear. The more comfortable she made him feel, the more the alarm bells rang.

Dammit all to hell.

When was the last time he'd had a home-cooked meal? When was the last time someone had cooked, just for him? Aside from his sister Alyssa and Lily Vieri—his best friend's mother and Alyssa's soon-to-be mother-in-law, which was still weird—Brady couldn't come up with a single instance.

Couldn't he just enjoy this, without all the running mental commentary? Fuck's sake.

By the time Joss turned the waffle iron off and guided them to the table, Brady was brooding and starving. Maybe if he took care of his gut, he'd shed the dark mood that insisted on clinging. He grabbed his fork.

"Eager much?" She grinned. "Just teasing. Dig in. It's fun to have someone else to cook for."

He nodded and took half a blueberry and half a chocolate chip waffle. He grabbed for the syrup.

"Oh, wait. I forgot something." She disappeared into the kitchen and returned with a bowl of mixed berries and a can of Reddi-wip. "The *pièce de résistance*." She waved her hand over the whipped cream.

"Seriously? Doesn't that make it dessert?"

"What? No. That's crazy talk." She loaded waffles onto her plate, drizzled on syrup, piled on some berries, and topped it all off with a crown of whipped cream.

Brady took a sip of coffee to hide an unexpected grin just as Joss swiped her finger through the white confection and stuck it in her mouth, sucking it off without seeming to notice he was watching. Raptly. Any number of sordid images flitted through his brain and the coffee stuck in his throat, sending him into a coughing fit.

"You okay?" she asked as she dug into her waffles.

He nodded and set about preparing his breakfast the same way she had. "All right. I'm going to trust you know what you're talking about here."

"Always a good plan."

Brady carved his fork through the mound of fruit, cream, and waffle, and took a big bite. He moaned as the flavors burst on his tongue—chocolate, buttermilk, a hint of vanilla, sweet berries, and sweeter cream. "You," he said pointing his fork at her, "are a waffle goddess."

She grinned. "And you are a man with much wisdom." She cleared her plate, grabbed and prepared another half-waffle, and dug in.

The urge to return the humored expression tugged at his cheeks. What was it about this woman? Here he was, the morning *after*, having breakfast with his supposed-to-be-*one*-night stand. What did he even know about her, really? A gut check called bullshit on that train of thought. He'd actually gotten to know quite a bit about Joss last night. But not everything. Like... "Know what I realized?" he asked, watching her eat.

"What's that?"

"I only know your first name. And since we're, you know, neighbors and all, I was thinking..."

Pink crept across her cheeks. A satisfaction he didn't understand warmed his chest. "Daniels. Joss Daniels," she said.

"Joss Daniels," he murmured. "Is Joss your real name or a nickname?"

She twisted her lips and nailed him with skeptical gaze. But all Brady could see was the smear of whipped cream on the edge of her lip. He reached over and wiped it off, his groin going tight at the feel of the sticky confection on the soft skin of her lip. "Little bit of cream."

"Oh." She wiped her mouth and dropped her gaze. "Nickname," she said, pushing her empty plate away stiffly and giving off all kinds of topic-not-up-for-discussion vibes. Interesting.

He let it go. "So, here's a question."

"Okay."

He finished his last bite of waffle. "How the hell does someone who looks like you eat like that?"

Her mouth dropped open. She let out an indignant scoff and whipped her napkin against his bicep. He caught it and yanked, tugging her half out of her chair. Laughter spilled out of her and the sparkle returned to those bright-green eyes. He hadn't liked the seriousness that had settled there when he'd asked about her name, and was glad he got her to smile again.

"So I like to eat. Sue me." She stuck her tongue out at him.

His hard-on took notice and he shifted in his seat. "Did you seriously just stick your tongue out at me?"

She crossed her arms. "I seriously did. And you deserved it."

Foreign amusement rocked through him. "I wasn't complaining. More admiring. And these were great, just as you promised."

She rolled her eyes, but the effect was lessened by the satisfied smile she wore. "You should finish them," she said. "They're best when they're fresh."

Brady eyed the remaining pieces of waffle and debated. He'd need to add another mile or two to his run if he loaded up on any more carbs. But, damn, it just might be worth it. He was pretty sure he could live on this meal for the rest of his life and die a happy man. "Fine. Twist my arm." He grabbed a quarter piece this time and loaded it with syrup and berries. He tilted the can of whipped cream, but nothing came out. Shaking it, he couldn't feel anything inside. "I think it's empty."

"Really? I thought that one was new. Here." She rose and grabbed the can, then shook it next to her ear. "That's weird." She pressed her finger against the white nozzle twice, but nothing happened. "I'll get a new one." She pressed it again.

Built-up whipped cream shot out in a long, fluffy stream and sprayed across her cheek, neck, and hair. She yelped.

Time froze for a long instant as Brady memorized the

image of Joss covered in whipped cream, her eyes and mouth wide. Then, miraculously, he burst out laughing. Deep belly laughs racked him until he had to push his chair back from the table and grasp his stomach. Her face went bright red. She narrowed her eyes and scowled at him, but even that was funny because of the whipped cream hanging off the corner of her eyelashes.

"Sorry. I'm sorry," he choked. He handed her a napkin. "Here." She ripped it from his hand, setting him off again.

Something cool hit him in the forehead.

His laughter died in his chest and he gaped up at her as whipped cream sagged across his eye.

And then he was in motion.

Brady dove for her and she screamed and bolted into the kitchen.

He grabbed her around the waist and hiked her against him. "Gimme that," he growled, reaching around for the can.

"No," she squealed through her laughter. A stream of whipped cream covered his arm.

"You little…" He made another grab and ended up with a handful of soft, warm breast. His cock came alive against her squirming body.

She gasped and attempted to twist away, sending off another stream of whipped cream that landed in both of their hair. They were laughing and panting so hard their words were more gibberish than not.

Funny as it was, there was no denying that his body was also reading something else into their horseplay. Something that involved cleaning her off with his tongue.

He swiped his thumb across her breast and groaned at the feeling of her rigid nipple pushing against the cotton that separated them. "Joss," he groaned, pushing his hips into her lower back.

She moaned and ground back.

He'd *so* not intended this. But, damn.

His mouth found a line of cream on her neck and sucked. *Delicious.* Her natural taste and scent of peaches mixed with the sugar to create an absolutely irresistible treat. "Even sweeter now." Her head sagged back against his shoulder and the feeling of her melting into him made his jeans painfully tight. "Tell me to stop," he whispered before dragging his tongue through the cream on her jaw.

"I can't." She shook her head. "I don't want to."

Brady growled against her skin, her words taunting him to give in.

He traced his fingers down her belly and Joss moved her arms to let him. When he removed the Reddi-wip from her grip and sat it on the counter, she grinned over her shoulder at him. He devoured her in a kiss, loving the sweet enthusiasm of her mouth, the slip and slide of the little metal piercing, as he undid the button and zipper on her shorts.

Yeah, he was going there all right. And, suddenly, her tongue wasn't the only thing he needed to taste.

He settled his hands on the waistband of her cut-offs. "Okay?"

She nodded her face against his.

Her jeans and panties fell to the floor. Together, they kicked them away.

"Turn around." When she did, he tugged at the hem of her tank. "Take this off for me, too?"

She only broke eye contact when the shirt passed over her head. Damn if he didn't feel her gaze right down into the tension filling his balls.

She dropped her bra from her shoulders, then stood nude before him. Long, tan legs, chocolate brown triangle of hair at the hidden apex. Flared hips perfect for gripping. A softly rounded belly curving up to full breasts just begging to be sucked. Her wild mane of hair was dampened here and there with whipped cream and just covered the swallow above her heart, but he could still tell that the colors of the tat were striking against her skin.

The room spun. "Jesus, Joss. You're stunning." He tossed his shirt to the floor, closed the space between them, and slanted his mouth over hers.

Her hands curled around his neck and pulled him in harder, tighter. Satisfaction roared through him. *Sonofabitch.* What was happening here? At least he wasn't the only one who felt this intense need, this unrelenting desire. What he didn't understand was why it all felt so *natural* between them. He'd never felt anything like it. Never allowed himself to get close enough, to stay long enough, to let himself do so.

Refusing to get caught up any deeper in his head, Brady pushed her back one step, then another, and lifted her to sit on the single stretch of counter without an overhead cabinet. Joss gasped and her nails dug into his skin, setting off a yearning to feel the pinch of her grip over every inch of his body.

He pulled back and met her gaze, loving the haze of lust that left her green eyes just short of focused, her lips wet and swollen, her chest heaving. "Lean back." He pressed a hand against the pale skin of her stomach. "I want you on my tongue."

Brady wrapped his arms under her thighs and lifted her so she sat nearer to the edge, then he dropped to his knees and placed a series of soft, sucking kisses on the insides of her thighs.

When her legs were shaking where they lay over his shoulders, he met her heavy-lidded gaze and licked straight up through the center of her. Her eyes went wide and her mouth dropped open on a whimper that had him straining against the fly of his jeans. And damn it all to hell but she was salty-sweet on his tongue. He'd thought of tormenting her with unending slow licks of whipped cream from her pussy, but in truth he thought the addition would detract from the intoxicating smell and taste of her. All warm and rich and female musk.

Supporting her lower back with one hand, he used his other to open her folds to his tongue's exploration. He alternated long licks with quick, firm strokes, and penetrating sweeps of tongue with deep sucking draws on the swollen nerves of her clit. His brain was cataloging those things that made her cry out or her hips jerk or her hand press down harder on his head. And even though he knew down deep he didn't need that information if this wasn't going to happen again—and it shouldn't, it really fucking shouldn't if he knew what was right by her and smart by him—he couldn't stop himself from memorizing every inch of her so he could please her again and again.

"Oh, God," she rasped. "I need you."

"Come on my tongue, sweetness, and you can have me any way you want."

She moaned as he concentrated fast, flat, hard licks against her clit. He looked up her body and found her beautiful face. Eyes closed, mouth open, expression frozen between pleasure and pain. Her breath caught, hips jerked, thighs went rigid.

Her eyes flew open as her head wrenched back, a long, low moan rolling out of her as she came. He lapped up her pleasure and drank it down, masculine pride surging through him and tightening his balls. Brady was on his feet and kicking off his jeans as fast as his painful erection would let him.

And whaddya know, the counter was the perfect height. God bless America.

He grasped himself and dragged the head of his cock through her folds, then froze. "Oh shit. Condom."

"Oh. Um. I don't have any. I haven't needed—" A blush spread over the flush still pinking her cheeks from the orgasm.

He shouldn't have been so happy to hear her recent sex life hadn't required a stash of Trojans. Especially since it meant they were high and dry at the moment. Unless he got dressed and limped next door. Urgent arousal kicked him in the lower back and had him curling his hips into hers.

"I'm on the pill though, so I'm safe. And, well, I'm clean. I've only had two partners, and both were long-term relationships."

Brady leaned in and kissed her. This shit was never easy to talk about, and he respected that she didn't hem and haw about it. He leaned his forehead against hers, which nestled his cock against her wet heat. An odd feeling of need that had nothing to do with his libido had him whispering against the soft skin of her face. "Shit, Joss. I've *never* done this without a condom." He cleared his throat. "And I just had a physical and got a clean bill of health when I returned stateside in June."

"We don't have to, it's okay."

Dammit. It wasn't even a question of trusting her. It

was *him* he didn't trust. It was him he could *never* trust. He was his father's son, after all—the anger problems that had earned him a one-way trip off the front lines proved that—and there was no way he was ever burdening a child with that kind of legacy the way Alyssa had been. So he'd never before given going bareback a second thought.

She pressed a soft kiss to his lips and gasped. Cupping his cheek, she stroked her tongue over his lips. "I taste good on you," she whispered.

Holy mother of— He rocked his hips, once, twice, sliding his rigid length against the velvet heat of her pussy. Glancing down, he watched himself and couldn't deny that what he really wanted to see was his cock disappearing into her, filling her, claiming her as his.

His? Where the hell was this possessive streak coming from? He never got all "you are mine" over his lays because he never, ever felt that way—his job didn't allow him the time and his nature didn't allow him the inclination. But, Jesus, it was there and then some with her.

Desire drowned out the confusion roiling in his gut. "I want to, Joss." He met her gaze, open and affectionate.

"I want you to, too. And I trust you."

He frowned, even as he took himself in hand. "You shouldn't," he whispered.

She pushed his fingers out of the way and guided the head of his cock inside her slit. "Saying stuff like that just proves I can." She leaned back against the wall and opened her legs to him, allowing his hips to come in hard and tight.

Cupping one of her knees under each of his arms, Brady groaned as he bottomed out, balls caressing the rounded cheeks of her ass. Skin-on-skin, the feeling was so much more intense, more raw, more real that he had to pause and breathe away the urge to plow into her, rush through it, chase what he knew would be an incredible orgasm so fast that it would be over before he'd memorized every moment of it.

"Does it feel different?"

"Hell yeah. It's insane, Joss. You feel so fucking good I'm afraid to move."

The corner of her mouth lifted in a small, sexy smile that had something in his chest stirring, too. "Move, Brady. I need you to."

As soon as he did, his brain went off-line and he was all sensation. The tight, white-hot glide of his cock in her slick channel. The soft quiver of her thighs in his arms. The soundtrack of her panting and moans mingling with his groans and rough exhalations.

If they'd have been anywhere but the kitchen, he'd have taken her to the floor, laid her out, and sprawled himself atop her. He wanted to feel the rub and press of their bodies moving and her arms and legs wrapped around him. He wanted his face buried in all that luscious hair. And he sure as hell wanted her nails marking his back.

Next time, his mind whispered insidiously.

There won't be any damn "next time." He shook his head, willing the combatants in his brain away. *Just this one time. Let me have this.*

Whatever else happened, Brady didn't want this to end without feeling Joss come around his cock. Propping one of her legs straight against his chest freed a hand to pleasure her, and he reveled in the gasping moan she released when he circled his fingers over his clit.

"Never come twice." She shook her head. "Never…"

"You sure? Because I love a challenge."

She half moaned/half laughed, then bit her lip. "Try it harder," she whispered.

"What, sweetness? Fucking or rubbing?"

"Both."

He nodded. "Gimme your hand." He placed her fingers on top of her clit. "Rub yourself for me. Show me what you like."

She peered up at him from under her eyelashes, and something told him she'd never touched herself in front of a man before.

His gaze dropped to where they were joined as he held up his end of the bargain and hammered into her, his grip tight on her thighs to absorb most of the impact, his dog tags bouncing against his chest. "So hot, seeing my dick in your pussy while you touch yourself. Just thinking about you getting off again is making my blood pound."

She rubbed fast little circles over her swollen nub. Her eyes clenched in tight concentration.

And then the tension exploded behind his balls and he was coming, pulsing, pouring himself into a woman for the first time in his life. Into Joss.

"Don't stop," she moaned, her fingers flying.

"Jesus," he ground out at the incredibly erotic sight, at the fact that he was going light-headed at the sheer force of his orgasm.

And then her pussy clamped down on him over and over and Joss unleashed a high-pitched moan that started low in her throat. Brady collapsed against her and swallowed her cry in a hot, wet, worshipful kiss. When her body finally calmed, his thighs were shaking.

"Holy shit," he breathed against her lips.

Running on pure instinct now, Brady stepped back and helped her down. Her knees went soft when she hit the floor, so he scooped her into his arms and made his way through the house and upstairs to where her bathroom should be. She was warm and pliant in his arms and the sensation of her nuzzling into the crook of his neck shouldn't have felt as good as it did.

The monster of his ancient anger stalked back and forth at the gates of his mind. But he was ignoring that mother-fucker for all he was worth.

Because, since he never allowed himself this—any of this, really—he had no idea how fucking good it could all feel, right down to her arms holding him.

He settled her on her feet against the wall next to the shower and reached in to adjust the water.

"Get in," he said when it was warm enough, his voice like gravel. "I'll wash you."

With a shy smile he found ridiculously endearing given their history so far, she stepped into the tub. A tattoo of a dozen tiny blackbirds took flight across her back, as if a flock was suddenly startled and rose into the air one by one, from the middle of her spine and disappearing under the length of her hair.

He stepped in behind her and traced the line of birds, pushing her hair over her shoulder so he could follow them to the nape of her neck, where they turned into a spray of colorful stars that ended just behind her ear. "This is beauti-ful." Something about the appearance of those rising, dark birds ascending to the stars tugged at his gut and felt inex-plicably familiar.

Warm, foreign pressure filled his chest. Goddammit. How could a feeling both ease his soul and trigger his fight-or-flight response?

"Thank you."

He turned her so the shower could wet her hair. "Tilt your head back," he said. And then he washed her, first her hair, then her body. And against all the lives he'd saved and terrorists he'd helped take out, somehow this moment, this connection, felt just as significant. The realization of what belonging felt like—of what others had but he never could—squeezed his heart in his chest until it was hard to take a deep breath.

So as he rinsed the suds off her tired, supple body, he allowed himself to be in this moment with her, to be owned by it, to allow himself this one exception to the cardinal rule. Because it could never happen again.

And, neighbors or not, from now on, he had to stay away from Joss Daniels.

Chapter Six

When she was dressed again, Joss went downstairs to join Brady, who had gone down a few minutes before to retrieve his clothes from where they'd left them in the kitchen.

She was nearly high on endorphins and damn happy about it. Geez. Her joints were loose, her muscles were exhausted, and her belly was full. She could probably nap the rest of the day and be entirely content.

She entered the kitchen and found him fully dressed and stacking dishes in the sink. "You didn't have to clean up." Stopping behind him, she wrapped her arms around his stomach. "But thank you."

"The least I could do," he said in a low voice. He twisted in her arms and stared at her a long moment, his features tight.

Her gut gave a weird little squeeze, but then he leaned down and kissed her, softly, in a way that made her feel adored, and the niggling sensation disappeared.

"Thanks for everything," he said.

She grinned. "Any time." And boy did she mean it. Any day that started with fantastic waffles and hot sex ranked right up there in her book. And the fact that it was with Brady, this kind, intense, and passionate man, well, that made it all the better.

He stroked his knuckles over her cheek and brushed his thumb along her bottom lip. His gaze made her think of reluctant good-byes. He dropped his hand and stepped away, clearly intent on leaving.

You're overreacting. She walked him to the door and forced cheerfulness into her voice. "So," she said, "if you need any neighborhood recommendations or help getting your place set up, just let me know."

"Yeah." He reached for the handle and looked over his shoulder at her as he opened the door. "Bye, Joss." His emotionless gaze scanned her face and he nodded.

"See ya," she said, her stomach doing that weird squeezy thing again. She gave a last wave as he stepped off her stoop and closed the door behind him.

Alarm bells rang in her head. After the incredible morning they'd spent together, followed by the amazing time the night before, she knew she was probably acting ridiculous. Still… Maybe she shouldn't have hugged him at the sink. She just felt so comfortable with him. It didn't make any sense, really, but there it was.

She had no idea what they were—or if they were anything at all. But even if all they ever became was friendly neighbors who had occasional crazy hot sex, it would be awesome. So. Everything was fine. *Don't go neurotic, Joss.* Right. Good plan.

Intent on some normalcy, she picked up her cell phone

and dialed Christina. No matter what, the past twenty-four hours called for some serious best friend time.

• • •

"What do you think of this one?"

Joss peeked out of her fitting room door. Christina lifted her arms and spun in the midnight-blue jersey dress. "That's the best one yet. You have to get it."

"Really? You like this better than the gray one? The cleavage might be too much." She tugged at the neckline, trying to cover the little bit of her breasts that showed.

Joss grinned. Christina looked like the preschool teacher she was: blond, sweet-faced, petite, and conservative. But despite their differences, somehow from the time they'd met at work, they'd just clicked. Best friends ever since. Christina had married last year, so they didn't manage to hang out as much as they had before, but she never could turn down a holiday sale at the mall.

"Definitely not too much. That's the one. I'm telling you. How about this?" Joss stepped out of her dressing room to show off the ankle-length black chiffon dress she'd found.

"Turn around," Christina said.

Joss smiled. The back was the best part. It had a cutout that framed her blackbirds perfectly.

"Oh, Joss. That is totally you."

"Couldn't wear it to work, though."

"True, but it would be a great date dress. If you get that one, I'll get this one."

The mention of dating sent heat to her cheeks. She turned away and peered into the mirror again. Twisting her hair on top her head, she imagined how she'd wear it to show off the tattoo. *Brady likes it down*. She groaned. "What is this? Fashion bribery?"

"Absolutely. You always ask me to go shopping and then I'm always the one who leaves with eight bags of loot while you go home empty-handed."

Joss chuckled. "All right." They returned to their fitting rooms, and she looked at her reflection. Taking a deep breath, she mentally prepared for the Inquisition. "So, speaking of dates…" She slipped out of her dress and arranged it on the hanger.

"Oh, thank God. I seriously wasn't going to be able to last much longer. What happened last night?"

Good question. She dressed, collected her things and stepped out into the hall, all the while replaying Brady's departure in her brain. She and Christina had the whole fitting room to themselves, so no harm in spilling here. "Well, the abbreviated version is that I met a guy and hooked up with him last night."

Christina's door flew open. "Define 'hooked up.'"

Joss opened her mouth to reply—

"You had sex!"

"Shh. Why don't you just announce it to the whole store, woman? 'Attention, Macy's shoppers, Joss Daniels had sex last night.' Oh, and this morning."

Christina gasped and her eyes went wide. "Good sex?"

Joss should've felt insulted at her amazement, but seeing as she was still kinda amazed herself, she didn't. Memories full of Brady's incredible intensity and hot, hard body rushed before her mind's eye. "Mm-hmm. *Great* sex."

"Holy crap. I have, like, fifty-two questions now," Christina said, stuffing her feet into her flats. "We need food for this conversation. Lunch?"

Food and spilling good dirt had always gone together for them. "Sure."

Fifteen minutes later, they were settled in a booth at a festive American chain restaurant off the mall food court, one shopping bag next to Joss and five next to Christina.

"All right," her friend said. "Spill. And don't leave out any of the good parts."

Joss recounted her night and morning with Brady, from the chance meeting when he'd caught her giving into a momentary pity party to the truck sex to the kitchen counter sex to his strained departure at her front door this morning. Even after their lunches arrived—a burger and fries for Joss, and a grilled chicken salad for Christina—her friend sat rapt the whole time, occasionally interjecting questions and sprinkling in a number of "oh my gods" and "holy craps" at all the right places.

"Do you think you'll see him again?" Christina asked.

"Well, I'll definitely see him, since he's my next-door neighbor." And, oh, goody, that won't be weird at all. "But, whether I'll *see* him, I have no idea. I don't think I imagined that he was off when he left. It was like the shutters had come down or something. I definitely wasn't getting a 'let's do this again' vibe, but, you know, I'm oversensitive about these things anyway." Joss shrugged, not as unaffected as the gesture implied. In fact, her gut had been heavy with the feeling of dread all day. She glanced down at her mostly uneaten burger. Out of nowhere, she recalled Brady's voice saying how he hated to waste food. She'd get it boxed to go.

Christina dropped her napkin on her plate. "Do you

want to see him again?"

Joss debated for a moment and nodded. "Yeah. Even though he's setting off red flags all over the place." She finished the last of her fries and attempted to keep her insecurities from swamping her.

"I think this situation calls for some froyo," Christina said.

"With toppings." She could always count on Christina to know just how to lighten a situation, or at least divert Joss from a downward spiral.

As they waited for the waiter to return with a box and their bill, Christina grasped Joss's hand. "Just give it some time. Neither of you expected this to happen, right?"

Joss nodded.

"So, just play it cool when you see him and follow his lead."

• • •

Christina's plan was sound, except the whole week passed and Joss didn't see Brady once. He was always gone when she left the house and not yet home when she returned in the evenings. Admittedly, his job had to be demanding. And she had been busy, too. The first week of the new school year meant extra hours setting up the center, filing student paperwork, catching up with the returning students, and meeting all the new kids and parents. Not that she minded. New school years had always filled her with an excited anticipation. As a child, the first day back to school represented an escape from the children's home where she'd mostly grown up. Now, even though it had been many years since she was last a student, September always gave her that same feeling.

This year, something new could happen. *This year*, anything was possible. *This year*, you could find a family and everything could be better.

Maybe she was being neurotic. Okay, *probably* she was. But it seemed more than coincidental that she hadn't run into the man even once.

It didn't help that out of sight did *not* mean out of mind. How many nights had she fallen asleep with the events of last weekend in her mind's eye? How often had she stared at her bedroom wall and imagined his big, hard body stretched out on his bed on the other side? How many times had her fingers served as a weak substitute for his? Sexual frustration, unending curiosity, and a bruised ego had been her constant companions.

So, on Saturday morning, Joss wasn't above gathering her dry cleaning and recycled grocery bags and heading out to run her errands just as Brady was coming out of his house with two other people, a dark-haired man and a petite brown-haired woman who was talking animatedly.

The September sun looked suddenly brighter, she was so glad to see him again. Both her behavior and her reaction to seeing him were a hundred shades of pathetic, but at least she'd finally have a chance to feel him out.

She opened the passenger door of her truck and dumped the cleaning, the bags, and her purse onto the seat. She didn't want to interrupt their conversation, but she had to at least say hello. Stupid, but she missed the sexy smart-ass even though it had only been a week. When she closed the door and turned, Brady had joined her in the space between their cars. He stood, watching her.

And damn did he look fine in a pair of beat-up jeans and

a navy T-shirt that emphasized the size of his biceps.

"Hi," she said.

"Hey." His gaze flickered to the couple walking toward the passenger side of his Rover.

She smiled at them, then looked back to Brady. "How have you been? I can't believe I didn't run into you once all week."

"Uh, good. My department has been gearing up for a big security exercise, so, yeah, some long days," he said, his tone stilted and uncomfortable.

Her stomach sank, just a little. "Oh. Well, of course. First week of back-to-school for me, so I get it." She felt the couple on the other side of his truck watching them, so she glanced their way. "I'm sorry to interrupt you guys. I just wanted to say hi."

"Hi," the young woman said. All at once, Joss realized why her features looked so familiar—she had Brady's eyes.

The man raised a hand and Joss nearly did a double take at how the brightness of his blue eyes stood out against his dark hair.

"Hey," she said.

She looked at Brady, and apparently her gaze galvanized him into action because he said, "Oh, Alyssa and Marco, this is my, uh, neighbor, Joss. Joss, this is Alyssa and Marco, my sister and her…" He frowned.

"Fiancé, idiot. He's my fiancé," Alyssa said, rolling her eyes. Marco chuckled and wrapped an arm around her shoulders. "Forgive him, Joss. If you have any brothers, you know they can be complete morons sometimes."

Joss laughed. She liked Alyssa right away. "I don't, but I'll take your word for it. Brady is a self-admitted pain in the ass though, so I do know that much." She grinned at Brady, who was watching the two of them talk like he was at a tennis match.

"Ah, you do know him then." Alyssa grinned.

"Yeah, a little. So, when's the big day?"

"Next summer, we think," Alyssa said. "We're still working on a date."

"Well, congratulations. That's great." She jingled her keys and smiled at Brady. "What are you up to today?"

"Aly's offended by my minimalist decor, so I guess we're going shopping." His eyes didn't quite meet hers.

"Brady, your house echoes it's so empty."

He shrugged.

"Well, good luck," Joss said, feeling more and more like an intruder, not because of Marco and Alyssa, but because of Brady's standoffishness. She'd only known him a short time, of course, but it wasn't a description she would've used for him before this moment. Clearly, he wasn't comfortable with her meeting his family. And, fine. He didn't owe her anything. A fact that made her feel even more stupid for the hurt sinking through her stomach. If she was reading him right, then she needed to go. Now. "I'll see you later." She stepped past him and waved to the others. "Nice meeting you."

Without waiting for their answers or looking back, Joss rounded the hood of her truck, got in and started the engine, and backed out.

At least now she knew where she stood.

Brady watched Joss's truck turn onto 36th Street and felt like a total dick. The initial bright, open expression on her face made it crystal clear she was excited to see him again after the week apart—which he had ensured by alternately working late, hanging with the guys at night, or running after he got home.

As he left her house last Sunday morning, unwelcome pangs of regret and longing had squeezed his chest until he could barely breathe. He'd felt his solitude more keenly after spending the time with her, and it had all just highlighted every fucking thing he could never have. He'd paced the length of his kitchen, scenes of what had transpired in *hers* tormenting him until that familiar red haze settled over his eyes. He'd nearly punched a wall. Instead, he beat the stupid out of himself with a grueling twelve-mile run in the heat of the day. Still, the annoying pull to see her crawled around in his brain all week, making him insane. Not to mention horny as all fuck. Seeing her again just now? Every bit of his desire, his impossible want, his anger roared back to life.

Watching her expression shift from happy to searching to hurt had just been icing on the cake. It was that last one that stuck in his mind's eye now. He hadn't meant to hurt her. Hell, the farther away he stayed, the better off she'd be. He'd just been blindsided by the force of the desire that flooded through him when he saw her again—not just sexual desire, but for the soft intimacy they'd shared afterward, the feel of her arms around his stomach, her whispering voice saying she trusted him.

He'd *never* wanted those things. With anyone. Never let himself entertain the idea. But one glance at her and they were all he could think about. And he had no clue what to fucking do about it. So he'd bit his tongue, swallowed the bitter, choking pill of his regret, and kept his trap shut.

And it didn't help that Marco and Aly were there. The only people who could read him as well as these two were 7,000 miles away on the other side of the world.

Forcing the thoughts from his mind, he got in the driver's seat.

Alyssa started in right away. "Joss seems great."

He kept his gaze away from Marco's, because his best friend would know instantly that they'd slept together. "Yeah, seems like it." He busied himself with backing out of the spot.

"You should ask her out." She leaned forward into the open space over the center console.

"I don't even know her, Aly."

"So? That's the point of asking her out. To *get* to know her."

Brady could feel Marco's gaze on him. *Don't look. Don't look.* He looked.

Marco wore a smirk that Brady's fist itched to remove. "Sure seemed like she knew you."

Brady rolled his eyes, glad driving gave him an excuse not to have to look at the two of them. And people said *he* was a pain in the ass. "We share a wall. Of course we've talked."

"Uh-huh," Marco said.

Fucker.

"So where are we heading, Al?" Brady asked, changing the topic and hoping it stayed changed. She rattled off some nearby furniture stores she'd found using her iPhone and they picked one.

The lot to the place was huge. And packed. Dread had

Brady strangling the steering wheel while he circled for a spot, which he finally found at the very end of a row. He parked, but didn't kill the engine. Instead, he looked over his shoulder at Alyssa, then settled his gaze on Marco. "Why don't we go see a movie instead? This place is insane."

Marco gave him a half smile that said, *You don't have a prayer*.

"You don't have any furniture, Brady. Let us help you while we're here."

"I can get furniture any time."

"But we're here," Alyssa said, pointing at the huge furniture store, exasperation coloring her voice.

"You guys have done enough of this lately setting up your new place. I'll do it later." They'd just moved into an apartment in a renovated warehouse in DC so Alyssa could accept a new event planner job she'd landed at the Washington Convention Center, while Marco was bartending and putting his GI benefits to use to finish his college degree. "Besides, how often do I have time to spend with my little sis?"

Marco grinned and looked away.

Alyssa rolled her eyes, recognizing his ploy for what it was. Now that they were grown up, he couldn't get nearly as much by her as when they were younger. "At least get a couch and a table. You don't even have a place to eat."

"Leaning against the kitchen counter works just fine." *Not to mention, Joss has a table—*

"What are you, fourteen?" she asked. "Come on." She hopped out of his truck and closed the door, ending the conversation.

Marco clapped him on the shoulder. "Good effort, man."

Brady shoved his hand off and killed the engine. "Why the hell didn't you back me up? There's no fucking way you want to do this, either."

Marco chuckled and opened his door. "I've learned to pick my battles with your sister. Now, suck it up and shop fast." The door slammed behind him.

Brady sighed and got out. When he rounded the rear end, he found Marco and Alyssa kissing in the narrow space between the parked cars. "Aw, come on. You two need to keep that shit to a bare minimum."

Breaking the kiss, they both smiled at him. When Alyssa caught up to him, she smacked his arm. "You know, we're getting married. We might even have sex someday."

Brady shuddered and shook his head. "I cannot believe you just said that. You are my little sister. In my mind, you are a totally asexual being. Fuck's sake."

She elbowed him. "Get over it already."

He glared at Marco, who held one hand up in surrender. He was holding Alyssa's hand with the other.

Brady sighed and looked away. Weird as it still was, he didn't begrudge Marco and Alyssa the happiness they'd recently found in each other. Marco had been like a brother to him since they were on the same peewee baseball team, and had been his brother-in-arms in the same Special Forces unit until he'd been medically discharged after they were ambushed last year. So Brady had every confidence that if anyone could take care of Aly, treat her right, and give her everything she needed to be happy, it was his best friend. Besides, after what she'd gone through growing up, it was right that she got to have a loving family now.

But that didn't mean he wanted to think about what

went on behind closed doors.

Two hours and forty-seven minutes later, Brady was the mind-numbed owner of furniture for his living room, bedroom, and dining room. Or he would be after it was delivered in seven to ten days. He made a mental note never to step foot into any retail establishment that had the word "superstore" in the name ever again.

He was somewhat mollified by the follow-up trip to the electronics store, where he picked out a laptop, Wi-Fi components, and a television.

"Food?" Brady asked when they were back in his truck.

"Food," Marco agreed. "Aly?"

"Yeah, I'm starving," she said from the backseat.

He took them to a Tex-Mex restaurant the guys at work had introduced him to. They got a table right away and dove into the chips and salsa while they read the menu.

After they ordered, Alyssa grabbed a chip and said, "So, once your stuff arrives, you can invite Joss over."

Marco leaned back in his seat and crossed his arms, hint of a smile on his traitorous face.

Brady scoffed. "I'm not inviting Joss over."

"Why not?" she asked. "She's really pretty. I love her pink highlights. Don't you think she's pretty?"

Actually, she's drop-dead gorgeous. Even if he never would've guessed he'd find a woman with pink-striped hair, piercings, and multiple tattoos attractive. "I guess. Whatever. Why are you trying to fix me up, anyway?"

She shrugged. "I don't know. It's just, you're home for a while and in one place for once… I just want you to be happy. That's all."

"Well, I appreciate that, Aly. I do. But I don't need to

date to be happy."

"Okay, that's true. But why *not* date?"

The waiter delivered their food and interrupted their conversation. Brady breathed in the savory spices and hoped it would stay interrupted.

"Yeah, Brady, why not?" Marco asked, amusement coloring his voice as he built a steak fajita.

Brady glared at him. Words shot out of his mouth before he thought them through. "Hey, Marco? How's your therapy going?" He knew he'd just donned his asshole hat, but if this was the way Marco wanted to go, two could play the game.

His friend scowled. "I don't know. How's *yours* going?"

Tension gripped Brady's shoulders and filled the space between him and his best friend. He had confided in Marco the real reason he'd been sent stateside earlier in the summer, so his friend knew his chain of command was making him seek counseling for his so-called anger management problems before they'd put him up for E-6.

But Alyssa didn't know. And he didn't want her to. Which Marco fucking knew.

"Wait, you're in therapy?" Alyssa asked.

"PT," Brady lied. "My shoulder's been giving me problems." He hated deceiving his sister, of all people, but she didn't need to be saddled with his bullshit, not when she'd finally found a little corner of happiness. And he didn't want to disappoint her by cuing her in to how much like their father he'd become. Hell, without the Special Forces, without the outlet of the rigorous training and punishing schedule the job entailed, who knows what he would've become.

"Oh, are you okay?"

"I'm fine. And, if you guys must know," he said, switching

the subject back to dating to get off the freaking lie, "I have no interest in dating because I have no intention of ever marrying. So there's no point."

Alyssa gaped at him. "Like *never* never?"

"Is there any other kind?"

"But why wouldn't you want to get married?"

He swallowed a bite of his *carne asada*, losing more of his appetite the longer this conversation dragged on. "Just because. For you guys, it's great. But it's not for me." He rubbed his forehead, a killer headache coming on. "Can we just drop it?"

When they got back to his house, Marco pounced on him the minute Alyssa went upstairs to use the bathroom. "What is going on with you?"

"I don't know what you're talking about." Much as Brady hated it, he really needed them to leave before he lost his temper. He needed a bone-pounding run to beat the asshole out of himself and screw his throbbing head back on straight.

"You've been irritable all day, and since when do you use my therapy against me? You know how I feel about that shit."

Brady knew he was in the wrong there. And he knew exactly how Marco felt about everything he'd been through this past year—the attack on his unit, which he believed to be his fault, the deaths of three of their guys, the medical discharge, and the permanent disabilities with which he was still dealing. But that didn't cool the red-hot rage boiling up inside Brady. "Yeah, and since when do you betray a confidence?"

Marco tugged a hand through his dark hair. "Dammit. I

shouldn't have. You're right. And I'm sorry. But that doesn't negate that something's up with you."

"Just drop it. Okay?"

Marco laid a hand on his shoulder. "Is this no-marriage bullshit because of your—"

Brady threw Marco's arm off him. "When I want your opinion, I'll ask for it, Vieri. Got it? Jesus." He scrubbed his hands over his face.

Marco's gaze cut hard right. Brady's followed. Alyssa was standing just where the stairs cleared the wall, watching them.

"Do I want to know?" she asked as she quietly stepped the rest of the way down.

"No," both men said, exchanging a glance. The one thing they'd always agreed on was protecting Alyssa. No matter what.

They said their good-byes, awkwardness choking the air between them, and Brady didn't even walk them out. The echo of the front door closing behind them still rang in the air as he took the stairs two at a time. Despite his headache, he changed into his running gear and raced out into the humid air of the early evening.

He glared at Joss's door as he passed her house, not because he was angry with her, but because he wanted to go knock on it so damn bad. Take her in his arms. Lose himself in her body.

And he resented the hell out of that feeling.

Because she deserved better than that. Better than him. So he looked away and broke into a full-out run.

Chapter Seven

By midday on Sunday, Joss had driven herself crazy with a laundry list of *maybes*. Maybe she shouldn't have hung around for a conversation with his family. Maybe he was just having a bad day. Maybe he never wanted to talk to her again. After a half-hour call with Christina debating the merits of simply confronting him and asking where they stood, she had just about convinced herself to do it. After all, as neighbors it wasn't like she could avoid him for the next year or two, and she didn't want that kind of stress and game-playing in her life even if she could. She'd rather just hear the brutal truth, know where she stood, and get about the unhappy business of picking up the pieces.

Joss gave herself one last mental pep talk, slipped on some flip-flops, and after what might've been a nerve-borne out-of-body experience, found herself standing in front of his dark green door. She lifted the brass hanger and knocked three times.

No answer.

She knocked again.

After a few moments, Joss peered over her shoulder to confirm his truck was there.

Waiting another minute, she finally knocked one last time, then crossed her arms and waited some more.

Muffled noises sounded from the other side of the door. It eased open.

Brady braced a hand against the jamb and lifted his face. His skin was somehow gray and flushed at the same time.

Her semi-planned speech went right out the window. "Oh, my God. What's wrong?"

"You should go, Joss," he said, though he slurred her name so it came out as "Josh." "I'm dying and I don't want you to catch it."

"Geez, Brady. I'm so sorry. Is it the flu? Are you throwing up?"

"Yes. Maybe the flu. I dunno." He sagged against the edge of the door.

"Do you have any medicine or crackers or anything?"

He shook his head and winced.

"Come here," she said, half stepping into the tiny foyer with him. She pressed the back of her hand to his forehead. "You're burning up. Okay, let me in."

"Josh—"

"No arguing. I know what it's like to get sick and not have anyone to help. And you have a friend here willing to give you a hand. Okay?"

"Okay," he whispered.

"Now, lie dow— Oh." He didn't have a couch. In fact, he didn't have anything. "Holy crap, you weren't kidding, were you?" she said. But he had a bed—she remembered him saying he'd had a mattress delivered. "Go upstairs and get in bed. I'll be back in half an hour with some supplies."

He nodded. "'Kay." He shuffled to the steps. Each slow, heavy lift of his legs appeared to deplete what little energy he had.

She unlocked his door and closed it behind her, then dashed next door for her keys and purse. Forty minutes later, she'd returned with everything she could think of to help him feel better. She unloaded the groceries onto his kitchen counter and put the cold things away in the refrigerator and freezer. *Wow. What a freaking guy.* The total contents of his fridge included an open case of beer and a pizza box.

And, good call on the plastic bowls, cups and utensils, because all his drawers and cabinets were empty.

She gathered the Tylenol, Pepto-Bismol, crackers and ginger ale and went upstairs. Tiptoeing into his room, she hoped she didn't wake him if he'd fallen asleep, but when a floorboard creaked under her step, he turned bleary eyes to look at her. "Hey," he said, voice gravelly.

"Hey." She tried to ignore the fact that he'd removed his T-shirt and lay there in only a pair of shorts, unbuttoned at the waist. He'd probably pulled them on to answer the door. "I got you some stuff."

"Don't want you to get sick."

"I won't. I never get sick." She touched his head again. His skin literally felt as if it could burn hers, he was so hot. "Let's get some Tylenol into you and bring this fever down." She wrestled with the child-safety cap, plastic seal, and ginormous wad of cotton and fished out two pills. "Take these," she said, handing him the medicine and a ginger ale to wash it down.

He pushed onto one elbow and did as he was told.

"Did you get sick again while I was gone?"

He shook his head and took another cautious sip of soda.

"Do you want to try some crackers?"

"Better not, yet."

"Okay." She stroked her hand over his forehead. His hair was damp with feverish sweat. "Be right back."

In his bathroom, she couldn't find a washcloth, but at least there was a hand towel. She soaked it in cool water and wrung it out, then returned to Brady. He'd collapsed back onto the pillow.

"This is going to be cold, Brady, but we have to get this fever down."

He gave a nod. She laid the towel over his forehead and pressed its length against his ears and neck. He sucked in a harsh breath through his teeth.

"I know. I'm sorry."

His eyelids sagged and finally closed.

Joss slipped across to her house and retrieved the thermometer, then on a whim she grabbed her book, too.

"I thought I'd dreamed you," he said when she leaned over him a few minutes later.

She smiled. "Nope. I'm here. And I want to take your temp. Open up." His eyes fell closed while the instrument beeped and the numbers climbed. This was really bad. She removed it from his mouth when it was done.

"What's the verdict, doc? Will I live?"

Ah, there was the smart-ass she knew and…liked. "It's 103.4, Brady. If this doesn't go down, we should get you to a doctor."

"I'll be all right."

"Just rest. We'll check again in a while."

"Thank you," he whispered, his eyes rolling for a moment before falling shut.

She pulled his door mostly closed, debated for a moment, then turned on the hall light and took a seat on the top step. If his fever got any higher, he was going to be in some serious trouble. She didn't want to leave him.

It took a few minutes to get comfortable—or as comfortable as she could get sitting on hardwood steps—but after a while her book sucked her in and she didn't notice her butt going numb anymore.

Joss wasn't sure how long had passed when Brady came stumbling out of his bedroom.

"Hey," he rasped.

She stood and tried not to stare at the miles of bare, muscled skin. "Hey. Any better?"

He lifted one shoulder in a shrug. "Gimme a minute." He disappeared into the bathroom and Joss prayed she didn't hear him throwing up again. Not because she couldn't stomach it—she worked with kids, for goodness' sake, so she'd dealt with her fair share of bodily fluids. She just wanted him to get better.

The door opened a few minutes later and Brady leaned against the jamb, dark circles marring the skin under his dull eyes, forehead furrowed in pain. "No puke. Yay."

She chuckled. "Want a Popsicle?"

His eyes went wide. "Aw, yeah."

"Go get in bed." She went downstairs and grabbed three. One for herself, two for him, just in case he was up for it. When she'd returned to his room, he was sitting up against a stack of pillows. "Temperature first, Popsicles second."

She handed him the thermometer. He patted the mattress beside him, indicating she should sit, so she took a seat next to his knees while they waited. The reading came back at 101.9.

"Better, but still not great. Fluids will help. Red, orange, or purple?"

"Red. Obviously."

She unwrapped and passed it to him. She chose the grape.

He moaned as he sucked on it.

Joss bit down on the smart-ass remarks flitting through her brain and settled on feeling satisfied she could help him, even a little.

"This is the best thing I've ever eaten," he said.

"Glad you like it. I slaved all day."

He swallowed a frozen chunk he'd bitten off. "When we're done, wanna have sex?"

Joss gaped at him. He waggled his eyebrows, and she burst out laughing. "You're such an ass."

Brady grinned and opened the orange Popsicle. He tipped it to her before giving it a lick.

"Do you think you could try some chicken noodle?"

He grimaced. "Let's see how these go first. I hate puking." He finished his seconds and slid down against the pillows. "You don't have to stay, you know."

"I just don't think you should be alone yet. You were at almost 104 earlier. That's into the scary range."

He nodded and turned onto his side. "Sleep more," he said, his voice already fading.

Joss took the opportunity of him sleeping to pop back over to her own house and make a quick sandwich. It wasn't like she could forage at Brady's place. Then she resumed her watch at the top of his steps to read her book and keep vigil.

An hour later, Brady was hunched over the toilet, throwing up a dribble of orange and dry heaving so hard Joss's stomach hurt for him. Finally, he flushed. "You should go. Get sick, too."

"Stop trying to chase me away," she said gently. "I'm staying as long as you need me." She trailed him into his room. Perched on the edge of his bed, she said, "Let's check your temp again." She slipped it from his mouth when it beeped. "Man. One-oh-two."

He stroked a finger against her knee. "Thank you."

"No biggie. Take these." She handed him more Tylenol and the ginger ale. "Just sip enough to get the pills down." His body had warmed the towel she'd given him earlier, so she soaked it in cool water again and settled it on his head and neck.

"I mean it. Above and beyond."

She shrugged. "It's what anyone would do."

"No, it's not, Joss. It's not."

"Shh. Sleep now and kick this thing's ass."

The corner of his lip quirked up. "Yes, ma'am."

She settled on the step again, her back none too happy about it. Before long, she finished her book. Outside the bathroom window, the evening light dimmed into twilight.

Brady opened his door and gave her a small smile. "All that furniture I just bought isn't doing you a bit of good, is it? Sorry."

His words resurrected the awkwardness she'd felt yesterday, so she just shook her head. "How you doing?"

"Maybe better. I'm gonna shower. Would you mind

making me some soup?"

She smiled. "Not at all. Still have a fever?"

"Might be gone. Feel me."

She heaved herself off the step and rolled her eyes when he weakly grinned. "You're a mess, you know that?" She pressed her hand to his forehead, then cheek. "Definitely cooler. I don't think it's gone though. Shower'll help."

He disappeared into the bathroom.

Joss made a quick trip to her place to eat another sandwich, heat up the chicken noodle, and grab a tray, then returned to his house and arranged a spread of things to take up to him—soup, a fresh ginger ale, and some cinnamon applesauce.

She carried everything upstairs and settled the tray on his bed. Footsteps sounded behind her and she turned.

Brady stood in the doorway, water droplets on his bare chest, hand fisted at the hip holding a towel in place.

Just…wow. Even sick he was gorgeous. Abs ridged. Chest solid. Shoulders mounds of banded muscle. "Sorry," she said, cutting her gaze back to the tray. "I'll just…" She thumbed over her shoulder.

"Stay right where you are," he said, a hint of amusement in his voice. "And I'll make myself decent."

"Er, okay." *He's sick he's sick he's sick*, she chanted to distract herself from the fact that he was getting naked five feet from her. The rustle and slide of fabric sounded loud in the room.

"Smells good," he said coming up behind her. He propped the pillows up again and sat against them wearing only a pair of gym shorts. "Have you eaten?"

Joss nodded. "I got a sandwich."

Brady grabbed the thermometer, took his temperature, and handed it to her when it finished. His temp was 100.4. "I think I'll live."

"Good." She passed him the bowl of soup and a napkin. Then yawned so big her jaw cracked.

"I'm sorry I've kept you here all day." He took a sip of broth.

She waved his apology away. "You didn't. I offered."

They sat in silence for a few moments. "Can I ask you a question?" he finally asked.

Joss braced her hands back against the bed. "Sure."

"What's your real name?"

Wasn't expecting that. She sighed. It probably wasn't easy for a guy like him to appear weak in front of someone else, especially a lover. Former lover. Whatever. So Joss decided to lay herself a little bare, too. Not her usual MO, but then none of this was, was it? "It's Jocelyn."

He took another spoonful of broth, mostly avoiding the noodles, carrots, and chunks of chicken. "And why were you uncomfortable telling me that before?"

She glanced down at her lap and released a long breath. "Because, to keep you from using it, I would've had to tell you I don't like the name. And to explain why, I would've had to tell you how the staff at the children's home where I grew up insisted on calling me that despite me repeatedly stating my preference for the nickname, which is one of the few things I can definitively remember of my mother—that she called me Joss." She lifted her gaze to Brady. "She died when I was six. And we didn't have any other family."

He sat very still, soup forgotten in his lap, looking at her. "Were you safe there?"

"There? Yes. The staff wasn't warm, but they weren't mean, either."

He frowned, went to speak, but then seemed to think better of it. His jaw ticked. "You answered that like there was a place where you weren't safe."

She released a long breath. "I had two foster families, when I was younger. The first only lasted six months when the woman got pregnant with twins, and they felt they couldn't keep me. The second lasted a year. It…wasn't a great situation."

Brady frowned and set his bowl on the tray. His hands drew into fists alongside him. "I'm sorry to hear that."

She nodded and yawned again. Between spending her day sitting on the step and baring her childhood experiences—something about which she never enjoyed talking, mostly because it seemed to make other people uncomfortable to hear it—she was suddenly feeling the weight of the day.

The mattress shifted and Joss startled when Brady's thumb caressed her cheek. "You look like you're going to drop. You should go get some rest now. I'm worried you're going to get this…whatever it is."

"You sure you're going to be okay?"

"Yeah. Just tired and achy. But better."

She pushed off the bed. "Let me at least get you some supplies for the night." Tray in hand, she returned to the kitchen, gathered fresh drinks, and laid everything out on his makeshift cardboard nightstand. "If you get bad during the night again, just knock on the wall. I'll hear you."

He managed a small smile. "Okay."

She stepped to the door. "I'll turn off all the lights downstairs and lock up. Feel better, Brady."

"Hey, Joss?"

"Yeah?" She met his gaze.

He shook his head. "Just…good night."

It was almost certainly not what he'd intended to say, but she gave him a smile. "Good night, sailor boy." She jogged down the steps.

"Kicking a man when he's down. That's harsh, woman. Harsh."

She chuckled to herself, made a pass through the first floor, and double-checked that the front door was locked behind her.

It was only nine forty, but she was beat. She trudged right upstairs, got ready for bed, and slipped under the covers. Mid-reach for the lamp, she paused and glanced at the wall.

She knocked on it, twice.

Knock, knock, sounded back.

Joss smiled, but just as fast the expression slipped from her face. She clicked off the light and settled into her pillow. A tear pooled at the corner of her eye and dampened the cotton.

She liked Brady. *Really* liked him. Her breath caught and she held it to keep the emotion from flowing that suddenly pressed outward from her chest. She liked him *too* much, given how few days she'd known him and how unclear his own feelings were. And that meant she was headed for trouble. With him, these feelings couldn't lead anywhere else.

So, she wouldn't go out of her way, and she wouldn't make it obvious, and she wouldn't be unfriendly. But, from now on and for her own self-preservation, she needed to stay away from Brady Scott as much as possible.

Chapter Eight

Brady finally cast off the plague and returned to work on Wednesday, though he still wasn't one hundred percent and had to drag his ass through the day. He canceled his therapy appointment and went to bed that night without even giving his daily run a second thought.

Thursday was more of the same.

In all that time, he'd only seen Joss on Monday morning, when she'd stopped over before work to check on him.

By Friday, Brady was feeling human again. Even better when, as he got home from work that night, Joss pulled into her spot just after him. He waited next to his Rover for her to get out of her truck, his body going tight at the thought of being near her again—no matter that he'd vowed to stay away.

"Hi," she said in a way that seemed almost shy. "Feeling better?"

She was wearing her hair down, just like he liked. Brady's

hands itched to thread their way into it. "Yes, finally. Thanks again for taking care of me on Sunday." Her help truly meant more to him than those words could ever encompass.

Maybe what she had done wouldn't be a big deal to someone used to that kind of treatment, but he wasn't. Not since his mom died of a stroke when he was seventeen, anyway. Afterward, he was always the one providing the care. For all intents and purposes, he raised Alyssa after their had mother passed. Not that he resented it one bit, but their father hadn't left him any choice—his wife's death destroyed him, and he lost his mind and every bit of kindness he'd once possessed in bottle after bottle of vodka.

Now, Brady was struggling to keep Joss's compassion from crawling deep under his skin and making him yearn for more.

"I'm just glad you're better," she said in a quiet voice before slipping by him. Her heat nearly made him groan. "Excuse me." Opening the passenger door of her Ford, she said in a singsong voice, "Peekaboo! There you are!" A moment later, she lifted a little kid out of a safety seat he hadn't noticed. Child on one hip and stuffed bag on the other, she closed the door and looked up.

Brady swallowed hard. "Er, you have a baby."

She chuckled. "Just for the night. One of the preschool parents is a single dad who works occasional evening shifts and his regular sitter went on vacation." She walked her fingers up the little girl's chest, setting off a giggle. "So me and Claire are having a girls' night tonight and next Friday night. Aren't we?" She kissed Claire's forehead.

"How old is she?" he asked, having absolutely no sense of such things.

"Twenty months," she said. "Claire, can you say 'hi' to Mr. Brady?" The girl tucked her face against Joss's neck. Every couple of seconds she peeked out at him, then hid again. "Gonna be shy, huh? Well, that's okay."

Twin reactions coursed through him. Admiration of how natural Joss seemed with the girl—completely comfortable, confident, competent. And fascination with how beautiful she looked with the baby in her arms. Something about the softness of her expression, the gentle sway of her body as she held Claire, the tender lilt of her voice—she was meant to do this, *be* this, someday.

His gut twisted. It was a ridiculous reaction, of course, since he'd already determined to stay away from Joss, but seeing her with Claire just reinforced that he should, in fact, stay away, because he could never give her a family, he could never be that guy. Not for her, not for anyone.

And that foreign warm pressure filling his chest every time he thought about Joss? Every time he remembered the close press and shift of their bodies coming together? Every time he considered the way she'd taken care of him when he was sick? Not even these feelings, these memories, could change the fact that he wasn't cut out for the life she held in her arms.

And she was.

"You sure you're okay, Brady?"

He choked down his regret. "Yeah, why?"

She shrugged, her gaze dragging over his body. "I don't know." Was she blushing? He swallowed hard, wanting to taste the heat with his lips, his tongue. Joss hiked Claire up on her hip. "Well, I better get her inside. It's dinnertime. Then bath. Then stories. Then bed. Right, sweetness?"

His gaze cut from the baby's big, toothy smile to Joss's face. She was looking at the girl with such affection. Did she even realize she'd just used the nickname he'd called her?

"Bye," Joss said.

"Bye," he murmured, his gaze tracking the sway of her hips down the sidewalk and through her door.

He spent the night nursing a few beers and attempting to watch TV. All he could really think about, though, was Joss's sweet taste and needful moans, her soft skin and tight body. The only thing that kept him from breaking his vow and marching next door was the knowledge that she wasn't alone. Around eleven thirty, a knocking sounded from somewhere. He peered out his screen door. A man was standing on Joss's stoop. Tall. Dark hair.

When her door opened, Brady ducked back inside, but stayed close enough to hear their conversation.

"Hey, Will. Come on in."

"Thanks. How's my girl?"

Her screen door closed and cut off their conversation.

How's my girl?

Surely he was referring to the baby, Claire. But the thought of some guy showing up next door, sweet-talking Joss, taking her out—touching her—ran ice down Brady's spine. "Fuck." Breathing hard, dark but satisfying images of what he'd like to do to such a man ran through his brain. He leaned his head against the jamb and banged it twice. It would happen. Of that, he had no doubt. Joss was too amazing of a woman to be alone. In fact, why she was single now made no sense.

You could be the one to ask her out. Not a quick fuck in her truck or on her kitchen counter. A real date.

Joss and the guy stepped out her front door, interrupting Brady's pointless thoughts. Standing in the dark of his empty living room, he watched out his curtainless front windows. The man cradled the sleeping child against his chest, while Joss went to the passenger door of her truck and removed the car seat. She put it in the man's car for him, then stood chatting with him for a few minutes before he left.

Brady melted back into the shadows when she turned toward her house. The desire to go visit her surged through him. He had the oddest sensation that his arms and legs and head might come free of his body, that he was fragmenting into a million pieces, and only the thinnest of frayed threads kept him in one piece—and that, somehow, Joss could hold him together.

Pathetic. No doubt his shrink would have a field day with that little gem of emotion.

Brady cursed under his breath and retreated upstairs.

He lay in the dark of his room and stared at the ceiling for a long time, willing sleep to come. His head was like a roiling sea, new and disparate thoughts cresting atop each monstrous wave, then retreating again as new ones rose. By four in the morning, struggling through the morass left him exhausted and strung out. He debated getting up and running to quiet all the shit, but finally he fell asleep.

He and Alyssa were sitting at the table before school, eating the last of a stale box of Frosted Flakes. Alyssa looked at him with her big brown eyes, desperately trying to eat her dry cereal quietly. They didn't have any milk, or much of anything else. The two of them just needed to finish and leave the house before their father woke up. Then everything would be fine.

"Done," she whispered.

"Good girl. Take your book bag and wait outside for me," Brady whispered back, setting their bowls in the sink.

Her face paled. "I left it in my room."

Brady gritted his teeth. "It's okay. You go out. I'll get it." When she hesitated, he smiled and nodded.

She tiptoed out of the kitchen and through the dining room, and ghosted through the foyer and out the front door.

Brady shouldered his own book bag and went the opposite direction. Pausing beside the arch that separated the living room from the back hallway where all the bedrooms lay, he peeked around the corner.

His father was sprawled on the couch, one arm and one leg hanging off. The TV had been on all night and now played a morning show full of overly cheerful people.

Brady held his breath and dashed down the hall to Alyssa's little pink bedroom. Her book bag was hanging off the back of her desk chair. He grabbed it and made his way through the house, not pausing at the arch this time. He was going for speed over stealth.

Turning into the kitchen, he froze. His father was standing at the sink, arms braced against the counter, staring downward. Instinct told him to keep moving, but Brady hesitated for just an instant.

What happened next was a blur. His father hurled one of the dishes from the sink. Brady dropped Alyssa's bag, raised his hands, and caught the bowl before it hit him in the face.

Whatever rage his father had exorcised in throwing the bowl boiled over when it didn't hit its target. He lunged. Grabbing Brady by the neck of his T-shirt, he slammed him against the refrigerator. His backpack cushioned the blow but his head snapped back against the freezer door.

"Think you're such a hotshot, don't you? Think the whole world lies at your feet. Yours for the taking." Joseph shook him again. "Well, let me tell you, kid. The world is shit and you're nothing. And you never will be."

He shoved Brady, hard. Brady tripped on Alyssa's backpack, lying on the floor, and crashed to the linoleum, his left elbow and knee taking the brunt of the fall. He'd protected the stupid bowl, though.

His father stepped over him, and Brady braced for... he wasn't sure. A hit, a kick. "Next time, clean up after your damn self," his dad said.

Brady scrambled up and grabbed Alyssa's pack, then ran out the front door.

She glanced from where she was sitting on the front porch. Her mouth dropped open. "What happened?"

Unsure of his voice, he shook his head, worsening the ringing in his ears.

"You're bleeding." Rising, she pointed at his elbow.

He wiped it away with his hand and managed a smile. "All better."

"Brady," she whispered, fat tears filling her eyes. "He hurt you."

Gasping for breath, Brady shot into a sitting position, the dream-memory still claws-deep in his skin. His stomach lurched. He bolted off the bed and just made it to the toilet in time.

He hurt you. He hurt you. He hurt you.

He threw up until it was impossible there was anything left in him. And then he threw up some more.

Jesus. Where had that come from? He hadn't remembered that moment in years.

He flushed and collapsed back against the wall next to the toilet. "No, dammit," he said, voice like sandpaper. "He hurt *Aly*." At seventeen, Brady had been big enough and old enough to defend himself. It wasn't too many months after the dream incident that Brady had raised his baseball bat at his father in a threat he had every intention of following through.

Afterward, Brady tried to keep Alyssa out of the Scott house as much as possible. And Marco's family had taken them in whenever they'd needed. Hell, it was Marco's dad who had driven them to and cheered them on through their baseball championships. And the high school graduation presents he received were all from the Vieris.

The one thing he'd known then was that he had to protect Alyssa, no matter what. And he'd done it. He'd been the protector.

But as he sat there on the bathroom floor in the gray light of morning, shaking and head pounding, all he could hear was Alyssa's twelve-year-old voice declaring him a victim, too.

Chapter Nine

Three loud bangs sounded against Joss's front door.

She jumped and her heart took off at a sprint. Joss glanced at the clock — it was only 8:00 a.m. — and saved the document she'd been drafting, a spreadsheet of local businesses to contact for auction donations for the center's annual fund-raiser. Who could it be this early? She ran to the door and looked through the spy hole. Butterflies tore through her stomach and a mixture of curiosity and worry rushed through her. She frowned and pulled the door open. "Brady?"

"Hey. Can I come in?" he said, sounding…strange.

She smoothed down the short nightgown she was still wearing, wishing she'd thought to grab a robe or a sweater. "Uh, sure. Everything okay?"

He brushed by her, the smell of soap fresh on his skin. "Yeah. I don't know. I just…" He paced to the dining room, surveyed the paperwork she had sprawled across the table, then turned back.

"Do you want to sit down?" she asked, watching him. She was beginning to get the very distinct feeling that Brady Scott was a way more complicated man than she'd first believed. That intense but playful demeanor she'd initially associated with him was only one part of his personality.

"No, I—" He turned toward her and stepped right in close. "Why did you take care of me last weekend?"

What? *That's* what he was so agitated about? She shook her head and searched for words. "Because you were sick, Brady."

"But why?" He leaned in until he was towering over her.

She took a step back. "Because you needed help. What is *wrong*?"

"Because I needed help," he murmured, brow furrowed, eyes dark. "I'm not some damn…weakling," he sputtered. "I take care of myself."

Annoyance with his aggressive tone had her straightening her spine and bracing her hands on her hips. "*What? Okay*, number one, of course you can. Number two, *never* have I thought of you as a weakling. Sometimes we all need a hand. And, number three, what the hell is the matter with you today?"

He stepped forward and, given his mood, Joss retreated. Her thigh came up against the arm of her sofa.

"I am not…" He shook his head and struggled to swallow. "I am *not* a victim."

A victim? Joss's fear disappeared in favor of gut-deep concern. The anguish in his voice resonated in a deep, dark part of her soul—the part that harbored hurts so old they'd been imprinted in her DNA. Damn if it didn't make her feel closer to him. However stupid that was.

Slowly, she reached out and cupped his cheek. "Okay," she said. She stroked her thumb over his cheekbone, the tip occasionally catching his long eyelashes.

After a long moment, she grasped his hand and guided him to sit down with her. His stare was hard and wary. Finally, he gave in and sat next to her, but he didn't drop her hand. Joss's heart gave a ridiculous squeeze at that.

His jaw clenched and his features appeared harsh and shadowed, but he was still the sexiest man she had ever seen. And he was apparently hurting. "Do you want to talk about it?"

His head whipped toward her. "Hell, no."

"Then what do you want? How can I help?"

His gaze bored into hers, and she knew the exact moment it went hot, because she felt his need down to her curling toes.

He closed the distance between their bodies and kissed her. His hand dug into her hair and fisted thick strands of it. Tugging her in harder against him, his tongue penetrated her, thrusting and twisting.

Joss moaned, surprised and overwhelmed by the taste and heat of his erotic assault. Gasping for breath, all the reasons this was a bad idea paraded through her brain.

"God," he whispered. "You always take it all away."

The desperation in his voice set off an ache in her chest that made her need to comfort, to soothe. How often had she had someone who truly *needed* her? It was a heady feeling, knowing you could ease another. She wrapped her arms around his neck and held him close, surrendering to the hot chemistry that burned so brightly between them.

His kisses grew more intense, more aggressive, stealing her breath and turning her liquid. She sucked hard on his tongue, once, twice, wanting him as frenzied as she felt. He groaned and held her harder, his fingers urging her not to stop.

Pulling away nearly killed her, but the desire to take care of him, to make this about him, flooded through her veins. She pushed against his chest.

"What—"

"Shh," she said, sliding to her knees on the floor.

Brady's dark eyes blazed as she settled between his thighs and unfastened his jeans.

"I want to take care of you," she said, tugging his jeans.

Expression awed and intense, he lifted his hips and she pulled the material away. His cock stood hard and thick. Joss took his length into her hands and stroked him. Leaning in, she slid his swollen head against her tongue—and her piercing.

He groaned, his eyes zeroing in on her mouth.

Satisfaction roared through her. She dragged the little metal ball from tip to root and back, wetting and teasing him.

"Take me in," he rasped. "Please."

Something about his words sent her heart thundering so hard she felt its echo against her eardrums. She sucked him in deep.

"Fucking hell," he bit out. His hand stroked her hair.

She crowded into the vee of his legs, her breasts crushing against his thighs, and worked to take as much of his cock into her mouth, her throat, as she could. The heavy weight of him against her tongue, the warm scent of his masculinity, the restrained urgency of his touch—her body was so hot and wet she never wanted it to end. She flicked her piercing against his hard length as she withdrew and plunged down again.

"Shit, that feels so good."

The gravel in his voice shot straight to the center of her. She reached between her own legs and pressed her fingers against her clit, aching for even the slightest friction. The contact made her moan around his cock, buried deep in her throat.

Brady released a harsh breath and slid his other hand into her hair. Her mouth still full of him, she kept her eyes on his as she sucked him in again and again. He looked at her with so much need, so much desire, her heart clenched.

He wanted her.

But did he want more than just her body? The freely given words of encouragement and praise, the soft petting of his hand, the fact that he'd come to her in a moment of such vulnerability—her heart insisted these were the actions of a man who *cared*.

Or maybe that was just wishful thinking.

She shoved the thoughts away and focused on him, on the wet slide of her lips and tongue over his pink skin, the teasing drag of her teeth over his hardness, the flick of her piercing around his head.

"Please. I need you," he bit out. His hips lifted, his fingers pressed. Joss sucked him in deep and hard and fast, hope flying. His muscles went rigid and a groan tore out of his throat. And then he was coming, hands tangling in her hair, thighs crushing her sides. She swallowed what he gave her and licked him clean. Resting her chin on his lower belly, she settled a hand over his heart, reveling in the sprinting beat she felt there.

He grasped her hand and pressed it harder against his chest. With his other hand, he stroked the hair off the side of her face, tucked it behind her ear. For a long moment, he seemed absorbed in these small touches.

Then he dropped his hand to the couch. Shaking his head, he closed his eyes. His shoulders sagged. "Dammit, I'm sorry," he said in a flat voice. His dark eyes opened and held an emotion she couldn't read as he reached to right his pants.

Joss sat back, bewildered by the sudden shift in his mood. "What for? I didn't mind—"

"This can't happen again." He roughly pulled up his jeans and fastened them.

His words were like a bucket of ice water. "*What?*" Like *she* was the one who started it.

"I just… This is wrong," he said, refusing to make eye contact and pushing to his feet.

Her stomach tossed as she rose. "Since when?"

"Since always."

Since always? Right, because he never wanted her. No one ever had. Why should this be any freaking different?

"Look, it's me, not—"

"Get out of my house, Brady." Stupid. She was *so* stupid. Here she was thinking this *meant something*, that he was here because he needed her. "Get out and don't come knocking again."

Without saying another word, he crossed the room and did just that.

Joss slammed and locked the door behind him.

Then she fell back against the door and slid to the floor. She pressed her hands to her mouth and fought back the tears. They fell anyway.

When will you learn, Joss? Nobody wants you.

She shook her head and tried to push the self-destructive thoughts away. But right now, she was nearly lost in those old emotions.

Joss heaved a deep breath and all she could smell was Brady. She couldn't stand it.

She rose and climbed upstairs. In the bathroom, she brushed her teeth ruthlessly, but she could still taste him, still smell him. She lifted the bodice of her nightgown to her nose. Pure Brady. She ripped it off and threw it the trash. God knew she could never wear it again without thinking of this morning. Then she set the shower as hot as she could stand it and stepped in.

Refusing to think of the morning Brady had washed her, Joss stood under the streaming water and forced herself to stop crying. It never changed anything. It never did any good. It just left her feeling weak and exhausted. And what use was that?

When she was done, she marched downstairs and parked herself at the computer. Nothing like a mountain of work to lose yourself in. The center depended on this fund-raiser every year, so the work was way more important than her hurt feelings anyway.

The only good that had come from the morning's fiasco was that she didn't have to wonder anymore where she stood with Brady. So it would be easy to stay away. Before her emotions got anymore involved than they already were.

• • •

By the following Thursday afternoon, Joss was debating calling Will and canceling on babysitting.

She'd been dragging all week. On Sunday she'd felt so drained she didn't leave the house once, not even to spy on Brady's furniture delivery when it arrived just after lunchtime. On Monday, she went to work. But each day felt harder than the last, especially because the week was jam-packed with planning meetings and outreach calls about the holiday fund-raiser. The budget allocation they received from the county only covered half of their programmatic expenses, so the center depended on the swanky fund-raiser being successful—and it was Joss's baby this year. After such an exhausting week, she just wasn't sure she had anything left to give to Will and Claire.

But she hated to complicate Will's life when she knew he didn't have an alternative. Plus, she really enjoyed spending time with his little girl. Unless she got sick or started to run a fever, she was determined to meet her commitment, and then crash all weekend long.

When the center closed at six on Friday night, Joss wasn't feeling substantially better. In fact, she'd been struggling with nausea all day. But she loaded Claire into her truck and made her way home through the traffic anyway. The gridlock seemed worse than usual, but maybe that was just because of how run-down she felt.

Relief rushed through her when she veered onto 36th Street. She'd feel much better after she changed into some comfortable clothes and had a bite to eat with Claire. She turned into her parking lot and her relief fluttered away.

Brady was getting out of his truck.

Thank you, universe. Seriously. Totally awesome of you.

This week, when the last thing she wanted was to see him, it seemed she couldn't *stop* running into him. Twice arriving home from work, once leaving for work, and once when she'd been lugging groceries in as he was heading out for a run.

Joss parked, came around the back of her truck, and got Claire and her diaper bag, all the while pretending she didn't notice him hanging around the front of his Land Rover looking like he might be thinking of talking to her.

Screw that.

Maybe it was childish. Okay, it *was* childish. But she avoided the whole awkward situation by walking back around the rear of her truck and up the far sidewalk to her front door. "Joss," he called, pushing off the car.

She fiddled with her key ring and adjusted Claire on her hip.

"Joss, please?"

Turning, she took a mental deep breath and reminded herself to keep her voice pleasant, and not to ogle his uniform. Damn him. "We're not doing this."

Brady frowned as his eyes scanned her face. "Are you okay?"

She glanced back to the door, hand fumbling at the lock. Finally, the key found the hole. She pushed the door open and took a deep breath before turning to him again. "I'm sorry. Weren't you the one who said we were wrong together? Well, I agree. So, please—"

"You don't look well, Joss. Are you—"

She sighed. "I've been taking care of myself my entire life, Brady, so I sure as heck don't need your help. Not now." She stepped inside and closed the door.

A half hour later, Joss's words came back to haunt her. She'd just prepared dinner for Claire—hot dogs and apple-sauce—when the smell of the cooked meat as she'd sliced it into bite-sized pieces made her stomach turn over. Violently. She dashed out of the kitchen, where Claire sat playing on the floor with some little plastic cars, through the first floor, and up the steps.

The vomit was on its way up before she got to her knees, and some hit the toilet seat and caught in her hair before she could center herself over the commode. Her stomach revolted again and again, because she could still smell the hot dogs.

"Ja? Ja?" came Claire's little voice, not yet able to pro-nounce Joss's name.

"I'm coming, ClaireBear. I'll be right there," Joss called out.

"Ja?"

Tears sprang to Joss's eyes as the gags continued. It was her fingers. From holding the hot dogs, her hands smelled of them. Still fighting back the retches, Joss crawled to the sink and scrubbed her hands until the skin threatened to come off. Then she held the soiled length of her hair under the running water and rinsed it out.

"Ja?"

"Coming, baby," Joss croaked. She wiped the toilet seat and flushed, then forced some deep breaths. Better. It was better. Okay.

But how the hell was she going to feed Claire?

Feeling ridiculous, she reached under the sink and grabbed a hand towel. She pressed the folded square of terry cloth against her mouth and nose and went back downstairs.

Claire was sitting at the bottom of the steps, stretching her little body up to look for her.

"Ja. Eat."

"Yeah. Time for you to eat. Come on."

Claire pushed herself up and toddled next to her.

When Joss grabbed the plate of food, her stomach rolled again. Though the nausea was uncomfortable, the barrier of the towel seemed to work, and she didn't feel the need to get sick again. She sat at the table and pulled the baby onto her lap. Claire fed herself the hot dogs, and Joss helped with the applesauce.

When Claire was done, Joss decided to leave cleaning the kitchen until later, scooped the little girl up, and carried her upstairs for bath time. While the water warmed and filled the tub, she removed Claire's clothes and diaper, and then settled her into the shallow water.

"Cup?" Joss asked.

"Cup!" Claire said, flinging water with her fingers.

Joss grabbed her stomach, which just wouldn't settle down. So much for never getting sick.

After having her hair and body washed, the baby was content to play in the water for a while. Joss rested her chin on her forearms and breathed through the nausea. With the way she'd felt all week, she supposed it wasn't surprising that she was getting sick.

Relaxing there as Claire filled and emptied the cup over and over, Joss's mind wandered.

She gasped and pushed upright.

Calendar. I need a calendar.

She fished her phone out of her back pocket and hit a series of buttons.

Oh no. Nonono.

Twenty-eight days from August 18th was…

"Oh, no. Oh, my God."

She was almost a week late.

Why hadn't she realized? Between work and feeling so crappy, her head had been in such a daze. But still…

Another series of buttons brought her to a pregnancy calculator website. Shaking fingers punched in the first day of her last period and then she read the information that brought up.

Conception: September 1

Pregnancy Test: September 15

First Heartbeat: September 29

"Oh, my God."

She scanned down the list of week-by-week dates.

Week 5: September 22

Tomorrow. That was tomorrow.

Due Date: May 25

She dropped the phone on the floor and grabbed a towel. Without even draining the tub, she lifted Claire, terrified that between the baby's slippery body and her own shaking hands, she would drop her. But Claire was fine. Joss wrapped a towel around her and carried her into the bedroom.

September 1st. That was the night of the fireworks. The night of…

Get the baby to sleep. Just start there.

"Okay," she whispered. "Okay."

Diaper and pajamas in place, she combed Claire's fine hair. They read a book together, then another. The girl's presence allowed her to hold it together.

When Claire's eyes started to droop, Joss laid her in the

center of her queen bed. Earlier, she'd rolled blankets into makeshift bolsters and laid them along three sides to ensure the baby didn't fall off the bed. Thank God Claire was such a good sleeper.

On autopilot, she pulled the bedroom door mostly shut behind her and retrieved her phone from the bathroom floor. She did, in fact, need help, so she made a call.

"Hello?" her neighbor from down the courtyard answered.

"Hi, Lisa. It's Joss."

"Well, hi, Joss. How are you? How's the new school year treating you?"

She tried to keep the panic out of her voice. "Oh, good, good. Listen, I'm very sorry to call out of the blue like this, but I need a quick favor if you're available."

"Glad to help if I can," she answered.

"I'm babysitting tonight and, uh, the baby needs something I don't have. She's asleep for now. Is there any chance you could just come sit at my place for ten or fifteen minutes while I run up to the shopping center?"

"You want me to come now?"

Joss nodded. "If you can?"

"I'll be over in two."

"Oh, my God, Lisa. You're a lifesaver."

"No worries. I was just Facebooking."

Joss chuckled and worried it sounded a tinge hysterical. "Okay. Okay, thanks."

They hung up and Joss went downstairs to slip on some shoes and grab her purse. Her neighbor from three doors down arrived instantly, dressed nearly identically to Joss in a pair of capri yoga pants and a T-shirt. She was a few years older than Joss, but they'd been friendly ever since Joss moved in.

"I won't be long," Joss said. "The girl's name is Claire. She's not quite two. But she's sound asleep, so I doubt you'll even hear from her."

"Don't worry. I babysit my sister's kids all the time. We'll be fine."

Joss wasn't sure how she got to the drugstore. The next thing she knew, she was standing in the aisle clutching her stomach and staring at about four hundred varieties of pregnancy tests. She bought three, one each of a different brand, just to be extra super triple sure that she'd totally gone and ruined her life.

By having a one-night stand. In her freaking truck.

Brady's more than a one-night stand, part of her whispered.

"Oh, yeah? Tell that to him," she mumbled.

"What's that?" the man at the register asked.

"Nothing. Sorry." He rang up the tests without any commentary, and she about choked when she saw the total. Thirty-five bucks. Oh, God, babies were expensive. They came with so much…*stuff*. How was she going to afford it all?

My savings.

The money she'd started to set aside for a house. Well, this certainly killed that idea, didn't it? But at least she had a little extra money tucked away. The rest she'd have to figure out later.

Back home, she and Lisa said quick good-byes that felt like five years were passing as the tests burned a hole in her bag, and then Joss went upstairs to confirm once and for all that she was as screwed as she believed she was.

She opened all three tests, read the dircctions, and lined them up on the counter next to the toilet. Annnnnnd of course she couldn't pee now.

She sat staring at the design in the tile floor for several long minutes. Finally, her body cooperated.

Test one. Test two. Test three.

She flushed, washed her hands, and glared holes in the plastic sticks.

I'm on the pill. Maybe this is just a mistake. Maybe my body is just out of whack from a virus.

That could totally be it. Right? *Please*.

Millennia came and went during the three minutes the instructions told her to wait. Except, it turned out three minutes weren't really necessary.

Test one showed two blue lines at about two minutes.

Test two gave her a plus sign a few seconds later.

Test three very helpfully provided the word, "Pregnant."

Joss stared at the tests. Blinked. Stared some more. Results were still the same.

She was pregnant.

What the hell was she going to do now?

And how was she going to tell Brady?

Chapter Ten

Brady was many things, but not often in his life had he felt like as big of an ass as he had ever since walking out of Joss's house last Saturday morning.

And he didn't know which made it *more* right—leaving her alone to live the life she deserved without someone as fucked up as him in it, or apologizing until she understood that being this fucked up was going to make him do stupid-ass things sometimes, but that he cared for her more than any other woman he'd ever known.

Jesus. Out in the field, out on the front lines, he was fearless and carefree. There, he knew who he was and what he had to contribute.

But with a woman? He'd never even let himself consider it. His father was an angry, bitter, violent son of a bitch, and so was Brady. The "little disciplinary problem" that had him sent stateside? Yeah. That involved punching an officer and inadvertently starting a bar fight. Made no difference to his CO that the guy had been manhandling a waitress who looked like she was none too happy about it. Because it wasn't the first time Brady had lost his shit, and it wasn't the first time he'd reacted fists first, brain second.

Now, he'd been branded a troublemaker and his whole damn career was on the line.

And the only way through the fucking morass was to confront his father and say everything that had been pent up inside him all these years. To lay it all bare. His stomach lurched and his chest went acidic at the thought. Especially because, after his little dream last weekend—the one that was now keeping him awake most nights—Brady's whole worldview about what his youth had been was threatening to tilt on its axis.

He'd *always* hated his father for what he'd done to Alyssa. Twelve when their mother died, she'd essentially been orphaned when their father fell apart not long after. But turns out that shit had happened to him, too, hadn't it? Not just Alyssa. Not once had he ever looked at it that way—or maybe he just hadn't *let* himself look at it that way. No matter how he sliced it, though, now he didn't know whether he was coming or taking a motherfucking trip to Mars.

And that meant he had no fricking clue what to do about Joss Daniels. Jocelyn. Someone who knew what a shitty childhood was all about if anyone did. The kicker was, she would probably understand the big, steaming pile of screwed-up that occupied way too much space in his head.

And why did that scare him even more?

Slowly, Brady became aware of crying—loud, persistent, and cranking up in intensity moment by moment. He concentrated on the sound. It was coming from Joss's.

Oh. Right. She was babysitting again tonight.

Brady reclined against his new leather couch and blew out a deep breath.

Fine. He'd go see his father during one of the next couple weekends. He needed to get that shit over with. Not just because the doc told him to, but because being wound this tight was going to put him—or, worse, someone he cared about—in an early grave when he inevitably lost it. So it was time to get control of his shit and man up.

But first, he wanted to talk to Alyssa. Damn, it had been years since they'd last had a serious conversation about what she'd—okay, *they'd*—gone through. In fact… Son of a bitch. The last time they'd talked about it was when he'd called from the Special Forces Qualification Course and learned she'd started going to the college therapist. Well, wasn't that a smack in the ass. No doubt he could learn a thing or two from his little sister. She was stronger than she looked and more courageous than he'd probably ever given her full credit for.

So, yeah. First Alyssa, then their father.

It was a plan.

Is that crying getting louder?

Brady pushed into a sitting position and listened. The baby's distress had escalated into a full-out DEFCON-5 wail. Last week, he hadn't heard a peep out of Claire when she was at Joss's. Now that he thought about it, he'd been hearing her cry for at least ten minutes and not only was it not getting better, it was getting worse.

The hair stood up on the back of his neck.

Joss wouldn't let her cry.

So either something was wrong with the kid, or something was wrong with Joss.

He was out his front door in mere seconds and knocking on hers not long after that.

No answer.

He knocked again and tried the knob, but it was locked.

"Joss?" he called, knocking again.

Jesus. He could hear the baby from here.

He jogged back to his place and made for his bedroom, where he retrieved his lock pick set from a pack in his closet, covert methods of entry being a skill in which all SF personnel received training. It took all of five seconds to pick the residential-style door.

"Joss?"

"Brady?" Her voice sounded thin and strained.

Brady sprinted up the steps.

She was hunched over the toilet, dry heaving. Her knuckles were white where she gripped the seat. "Can you please… get…Claire? I…accidentally woke her," she said, fighting back gags.

Get Claire?

"Oh. Okay." Brady hesitated to leave Joss, but then turned to her bedroom door and pushed it open. Slowly. Tentatively.

Claire sat in the middle of the bed, eyes clenched, mouth open in a shriek, red face apparent even in the dimness of the small lamp.

"Hi, Claire. Um…it's okay."

She wailed louder. Those were some serious lungs.

He approached her slowly, like she was a suspect or an enemy informant.

Actually, he'd be much more competent handling either of those.

At the bed, Brady held out his hands to try to quiet her down. "Shh. No need to cry. It's okay."

The wailing continued.

What now?

"Get Claire." That's what Joss had said. As in… *Oh, right*.

He leaned forward, slid his hands under her arms, and lifted her. For a moment, he held her straight out from his body, her little legs pumping and kicking. Her screams seemed to say, *Hey, idiot, you don't know what the frack you're doing.*

And she was right, seeing how she was the first baby he'd ever held and all.

The image of the way Joss carried her came to mind. Brady brought Claire against his chest. It was truly amazing that something that weighed so little could make this much noise.

He bent his knees a couple of times and bounced her. He tried to think of something to say. Or, better, sing. For the life of him, he couldn't think of a single kids' tune. *Think, Scott, think. The enemy is approaching and the attack will commence in T-10 seconds.*

"Uh…uh…*First to fight for the right, And to build the Nation's might, And the army goes rolling along, Proud of all we have done, Fighting till the battle's won, And the army goes rolling along.*"

Claire's wails lessened to a series of hitching breaths and uncertain whines. Brady smiled.

"*Then it's hi, hi, hey, The army's on its way, Count off the cadence loud and strong….*"

She yawned so big Brady could see her lungs. It wasn't a rousing endorsement, but at least she wasn't crying anymore.

Brady put his hand on her back and patted her a couple of times while he continued to sing.

Yeah. Okay. He was doing this.

Claire looked at him and burped.

He stared at her a long moment, then grinned. "Good one. A solid B-plus, at least. With a little training, you could be doing A work in no time."

"Army theme songs and burp training. That's all you could come up with, sailor boy?"

Brady turned and found Joss leaning against the door-jamb, face pale, one hand clutched around her stomach. Actually, he was pretty sure the wall was all that was holding her up. She gave him a small smile.

"What's the matter?"

She closed her eyes and heaved a deep breath. "Just a very bad upset stomach. I made the mistake of trying to clean up the dinner mess after the nausea started, and then I tripped and fell running up the steps and woke Claire up with the latest round of…" She thumbed over her shoulder.

"Shit, Joss, are you okay? I knew you were gonna catch what I had."

"I'll be okay." Her gaze dropped to the floor. "And that was two weeks ago. I don't have what you had, trust me. And, uh, language, please."

"Huh?"

She looked at Claire.

"Oh. Oh, sorry. I suck at this. Sorry."

"You don't. You got her to stop crying, didn't you?" She pushed off the wall and immediately swayed.

Brady rushed forward and grabbed Joss's shoulder, hauling her against his chest. It hadn't been his intention—holding the baby with the other arm threw off his balance. And for a moment, he held the two girls tight in his arms, like…like they were…

He couldn't bring himself to finish the thought.

"Lie down," he ordered, the words coming out harsher than he intended.

Hurt flickered through Joss's green eyes. "Sorry," she whispered, moving gingerly into a sitting position on the edge of the bed. "Here, give her to me. The two of us can rest together until her dad arrives."

He frowned. "And what time is that?"

"Should be about eleven thirty, unless he gets caught at an incident."

He glanced at his watch. That was still ninety minutes away. "But what happens if you get sick again?"

"I'll manage. It's not that long." Joss's gaze narrowed at him. "Hey, how did you get in here anyway?"

The question caught him off guard. "Uh." His gaze followed Claire's hands, gripping and pulling at his watch. "I picked the lock."

Her jaw dropped open. "You *what*?"

"What?"

"Brady, you can't just go around picking locks."

He nailed her with a no-shit stare. "Obviously. But I could hear Claire crying through my wall. And I knew there was no way you'd let it go on that long. So, when you didn't answer the door, I did what needed to be done. Be glad I used a pick and not my shoulder or you'd have a door to replace right now."

After a few moments, her expression softened. "Okay. I see your point. I guess…thank you."

His ire died down. "You're welcome."

"Ja. Eat?" Claire said.

Brady frowned at the kid, and then at Joss. "Translate."

"She's hungry."

"You got *that* from *that*?" He nodded at the kid.

Joss chuckled, but it was a tired, hollow sound. She swung her legs off the bed.

He held out a hand. "Whoa, whoa. Where are you going?"

"She's hungry," she said like it was obvious.

Brady's mind flew for a solution that resulted in both of the women getting what they needed. And the only one he could come up with involved him playing babysitter. God help the baby. "Aw, shit—I mean… Sorry. Sorry. Just, uh, tell me what to feed her. Maybe I can handle it without, you know, dropping her on her head or something."

Joss pressed her lips together and tried not to smile. "You think?"

"I give us a fifty-fifty shot."

"In the cabinet next to the fridge there are Goldfish. See if those will work."

He grimaced. "She eats goldfish?"

Joss rolled her eyes. "They're crackers."

"Fish crackers?"

"Oh, my *God*. They're cheddar crackers in the shape of fish."

"If they're cheese crackers, why are they shaped like fish?"

Joss flopped back against the bed and curled into a ball.

"Right. Goldfish it is." He carried Claire out of the room and down the steps, feeling the whole way like maybe he should hold onto the railing.

"Ja. Nigh-nigh," Claire said, big blue eyes looking at him.

"Uh, sure." He knew three languages, and none of them were helping him out right now.

In the kitchen, the remnants of an earlier meal lay on the counter and dishes filled the sink. Brady stopped at the cabinet closest to the fridge and found the package of Goldfish crackers. Claire held her hands out. "Oh, yeah? Like these?"

"Eat."

That one Brady understood. He sat her on the counter and poured some out next to her. She grabbed a handful and stuffed them in her mouth.

"Why are they smiling?" he asked her.

Claire just looked at him and ate her crackers. "Ding," she said.

"Er…come again?"

"Ding."

"I'm sorry, I don't…" He shook his head and debated asking Joss what "ding" might mean, but then Claire mimicked drinking from a cup.

"*Oh*, drink? Do you want a drink?"

"Ding." Claire knocked three goldfish on the floor while grabbing another handful.

"Dings we can do," Brady said, opening cupboards looking for Joss's cups. *Bingo*. He grabbed a glass and turned to the sink to fill it.

When he turned around, Claire was leaning way far over the counter to look at the dropped crackers.

Brady dashed across the narrow kitchen and caught her with his palm. Water sloshed over the edge of the glass and ran over his hand and down his shirt.

"Uh-oh," Claire said.

"Why is it always possible to understand a woman criticizing you?"

"Uh-oh," Claire repeated, pointing at the wet trail.

"Yeah, yeah, it's only water."

Claire giggled and ate more fish.

Brady popped a few in his mouth. "Mmm, not bad." Hey, these were kinda addictive. He ate a few more.

Finally, she seemed to be done. Brady returned the package to the shelf and picked her up off the counter. Her pants felt damp on the bottom. *Aw, hell no.*

Debating, he went upstairs, totally intent on a handoff. He turned into Joss's room. "Hey, uh, I think—"

She was curled into a fetal position, a pillow balled up against her stomach, softly snoring.

"Ja nigh-nigh," Claire said in a loud, happy voice.

This time Brady understood her. "Yes, so shh," he whispered. Now what was he going to do? On the long dresser, he spied the baby's bag he remembered Joss carrying and grabbed it, then took Claire downstairs again.

He looked at his watch. Nearly ten forty-five. Forty-five minutes until the parental unit should arrive. He could handle that, right? No problem.

"Now, where should we deal with the wet bottom issue?" He kneeled on the living room carpet and laid Claire down. She immediately turned to her side. "Whoa, slow down there." He rolled her back over and gave her a once-over.

Sooo, start with the pants. Brady tugged down the pink and white bottoms and laid them aside. The big puffy diaper had cartoon characters on it, telling Brady what he had to look for in the bag. He grabbed a new one and sat it next to his knee.

"Okay, Claire. We're gonna remove this pee bomb you got here."

He lifted the Velcro tabs and pulled it out from under her. Damn, the thing weighed five pounds if it weighed anything.

"That's impressively disgusting." He held it up for a minute, trying to figure out where to put it. He stretched and set it aside on the floor.

Claire flopped to the side again. "Hey, no, no. Getcha butt back over here." She giggled when he rolled her over.

Brady unfolded the new diaper and laid half under her and pulled the other half up between her legs. "How does this thing close?" Where were the tabs on this one? He pulled it back out again and examined it further. *Ooooooh.* He finished unfolding the leg hole pieces, turning the long thin rectangle into an hourglass shape.

Before long, he had it on her. Sorta. "You think this is supposed to be this loose?" He shrugged and figured the pajamas pants would help hold it in place. Putting them on her was like wrestling an eel, but soon he had the kid all put together again.

"See? Knew we could handle that. So, uh, now what?

An idea occurred to him and he fished his phone out of his pocket. "Do you like *Angry Birds*, Claire? Everybody likes *Angry Birds*."

He pulled her into his lap and amused her with everything from video games to music to photos he'd taken in Afghanistan.

Eventually, there was a knock on the door.

Brady left the phone in Claire's chubby hands and answered, right away recognizing the man from the previous week. The big guy frowned. "Uh, I'm Will. Joss is babysitting my daughter," he said.

"I'm Brady. A friend of Joss's. She got sick about two hours ago and asked me to help out until you got here. Come on in."

"Dada," Claire cried, holding up her hands.

"Hey, baby girl," he said, his voice doing a 180-degree change. He picked the girl up, shouldered the diaper bag, and turned to Brady. "This yours?"

He accepted his phone back. "Thanks."

"Is Joss okay?"

"Yeah, stomach virus or something. She'll be fine. She felt horrible to not be able to watch Claire," he felt the need to add.

Will nodded. "Sounds like her." He pulled some folded bills from a pocket. "Give this to her for me?"

Brady laid the cash on the coffee table. "I'll make sure she gets it."

Will glanced up the steps. Ten to one odds this guy was interested in Joss. Why wouldn't he be?

"Tell her I'll give her a call tomorrow. To say thanks," Will said as he crossed to the door.

When the guy stepped out, Brady read "ACFD" in bold letters on the back of his navy shirt. "Will do," he made himself say. Guy had to be a fucking firefighter, didn't he? Someone like that was damn hard to hate.

Will leaned back in. "I need Claire's car seat."

"Oh." Brady gestured him forward. "Let me see if her truck's open." He figured he could always pick the lock if he had to. But, no, it was open. He frowned at that fact as he wrestled the car seat from the seat belt. Babies really ought to come with instructions.

Finally, Will and Claire were gone. He returned to Joss's place and debated what to do. He settled on leaving her a note and headed to the kitchen to look for a pen and some paper. First thing he saw when he walked in was the dinner mess. Ten minutes later, he had that all cleaned up, and then he spied a notepad and pen in a basket by the phone.

He scrawled out a note and took it upstairs. For a long moment, he stared down at Joss. A strand of pink curled onto her cheek. Brady pushed it back and stroked her face, her neck.

In that moment, what he wanted more than anything was to shut out the light, crawl into bed with her, and pull her back against his front. And just sleep. In the morning, well, they could act out some other fantasies, too...

Maybe—and it was a big damn maybe—after he had it out with his father, he'd consider letting himself act on thoughts like that. But, for now, he was in no position to take care of anyone else until he started taking care of himself.

Chapter Eleven

Knock on the wall if you need me.

Joss held Brady's note in her hand and read the words over and over again.

If only it were that simple.

She flopped onto her back and lay thinking so long the room brightened with early morning sun. Finally, she flipped the covers off her body, lifted her T-shirt, and stared down at her flat belly.

Pregnant. She'd always dreamed of having children of her own. But in those dreams, she'd never been a single parent.

Last night, Brady had totally covered her butt. Even though he'd been awkward and uncomfortable handling Claire, he'd still done a great job stepping in and helping out. But that in no way meant he'd be enthusiastic about having a baby of his own.

After all, he didn't even want the baby's mother.

On a sigh, Joss pushed herself out of bed. A strange

sensation of vertigo made her head swim for a moment, but at least she wasn't nauseous. She treated herself to a long shower, threw her hair into a ponytail, and got dressed.

Maybe she could get in to the doctor's for a pregnancy test today. Even though she had a trio of 99.9-percent-accurate results telling her she was now eating for two, she didn't even want to broach the subject with Brady until she'd gotten final confirmation from her doctor.

She made the call and got approval to go to the lab for the urine and blood tests, but would have to wait until Wednesday before she could see the doctor. Fine. She could wait. It wasn't like she didn't already know the answer.

In the kitchen, she stopped short as her brain tried to determine what was out of place. That was it. *Nothing* was out of place. The counters were clean. The dishes were washed.

Brady.

Her heart squeezed in her chest.

She chanced two pieces of toast for breakfast and reveled in her still-settled tummy.

Before she left for the lab, there was one thing she needed to do—she retrieved Brady's note from her nightstand and wrote a quick note of her own on the back:

Thanks for all your help last night. I really appreciated it.

~J

There. Short. Sweet. To the point.

Outside, she found his truck gone and was glad for it. The last thing she was up for was another round with Brady—of fighting *or* anything else. She slipped the note into his mail slot and headed out to pee in a cup. Joy.

Afterward, she called Christina and asked her to come over. She didn't want to say anything to Brady yet, but she sure as hell needed to get some of this off her chest before she exploded. Some serious girl time was in order.

An hour later, Christina arrived with sustenance in hand—a large pepperoni pizza and two pints of Ben & Jerry's.

"You are my favorite person ever," Joss said as she unburdened Christina of some of her load.

"Of course I am."

They placed everything on the coffee table, and then retrieved drinks, plates, napkins, and the all-important spoons from the kitchen. Christina settled onto one end of the couch. Joss took the other.

Christina turned to her with an expectant gaze. "So, are you going to spill whatever's bothering you? Or are we going to eat and spend two hours watching a movie before you work yourself up to it?"

"No stalling. Not this time. I need to talk." Joss reached for the spoon and her pint of chocolate chip cookie dough.

"Oh, my. We're going dessert first?" She retrieved her tub of chocolate fudge brownie. "This must be serious."

Joss savored the sweet creaminess of her favorite ice cream. "It is," she finally said. Her stomach flip-flopped at the idea of giving voice to her predicament, and threatening tears stung the back of her eyes. She blinked, refusing to start out a blubbering mess or else she'd never get the words out.

"Oh, honey, you can tell me," Christina said, scooting closer. She sat cross-legged right next to Joss.

Joss took a long breath, and let the words fly. "I'm pregnant."

Christina's eyes went wide and her jaw dropped open. "What? How? I mean…what? I mean…" She shook her head, bewilderment pouring off her. "*Who?*"

Making that admission had been easier than she'd expected. "That guy I met Labor Day weekend."

Her friend's eyes went wider yet and she waved her hand to continue. "The one-night-stand guy?"

She swallowed a bite of cookie dough. "Yes."

"Holy crap, Joss. I… We might need more ice cream. Or wine. Well, wine for me."

She chuckled at Christina's deer-in-the-headlights expression. It wasn't like she was the one who was pregnant. Yet, how good laughing felt right now.

"Well, okay, let's take this all apart," Christina said. "First, are you okay? Emotionally? Physically? Have you seen a doctor? How far along are you?"

"Whoa. Slow down." Joss steeled herself with another bite of ice cream. "I think I'm five weeks along. I went to the lab this morning and I see the doctor on Wednesday. I was sick as a dog last night, which is what finally clued me in. With feeling so crappy all week, I hadn't realized how late I was until I actually counted it out." She shoved in another spoonful. It was like each bite gave her more and more courage. "Emotionally…I don't know. I'm all over the place."

"You're still processing all this."

"Yeah."

Christina pointed her spoon at Joss. "Does the guy… uh—"

"Brady."

"Brady. Right. Does he know yet?"

Joss frowned. "No. I wanted to wait until the doctor confirmed it, which I know she will. But I'm not expecting Brady to be happy about this, so…" She poked at her ice cream.

"Have you talked to him since that morning?"

Talked…and other things. "A few times, yeah. I thought he was interested for a while, but then…" Joss shrugged. "He made it clear he's not."

"And, are you interested in him? I mean, beyond the couple of times you guys…you know…"

Joss fell back against the couch and sighed.

"Oh." Christina set her ice cream aside and grasped one of Joss's hands. "Maybe he'll come around, you know?"

Joss gave her fingers a squeeze. "I don't know. Maybe," she said, even though in her heart of hearts, she didn't think so. On top of everything else, a baby didn't fit in well with his career. Especially an unplanned one. Joss set her ice cream on the table. "You know, growing up like I did, I've always wanted children, a big family, the whole Norman Rockwell thing. This just isn't what I expected. It isn't how I thought it would be."

Christina gave her a small smile and wrapped her arms around Joss's shoulders. Foreheads touching, she said, "Sometimes the best things never are."

. . .

Brady arrived home on Wednesday evening feeling better about his latest visit to his therapist than he ever had before. Not that he liked talking about this shit, because he didn't—he hated it. But there was at least a little satisfaction in the doc's comment that his willingness to consider he might've been victimized, too, represented real progress. The idea still settled in Brady's stomach like a pile of nails rolled in crushed glass, but he could find his way to understanding how someone might look at his past and come to that conclusion. For once, Brady came away from the appointment feeling like it hadn't been a complete waste of time.

He shuffled through the bills and junk mail and tossed the pile to the kitchen counter, then headed upstairs to get changed for a run. Joss's thank-you note lay crinkled on his nightstand. He picked it up and turned it around in his hands. The only time he'd seen her after Friday night was last night after work. She'd arrived home when he was heading out for a run. And it was clear from her one-word answers and lack of eye contact that, despite the undeclared truce between them when she'd taken sick, Joss hadn't forgiven him for being such a dick.

And why should she?

He hadn't forgiven himself.

One thing at a time. Maybe after he'd had it out with his father, he could… He didn't even know. But hope slinked through his brain, tempting him, drawing him out. Such a damn dangerous emotion. Brady had never before put any stock in hopes and dreams. His feet were planted squarely on the ground. Always had been. And the ground was often littered with the ugly, brutal truth of real life.

Still, between the memory of how much Joss had comforted him before he'd gone and ruined everything that morning and the therapist's encouragement, giving into even a little hope was damn near irresistible.

Brady dropped the note back on his nightstand, changed for his run, and made a pit stop in the bathroom.

A knock sounded at his front door.

He flushed and washed his hands as whoever was at the door knocked again, louder this time. "Keep your pants on," he muttered, then double-timed it down the steps.

Maybe it was Joss…

He pulled the door open.

Alyssa and Marco stood on the other side, Marco hold-ing the screen door open with his back. Alyssa looked…

"What's wrong?" Brady asked, ushering them in.

He shook hands with Marco, and the seriousness in the guy's blue eyes sank like a rock in Brady's gut.

"Al—"

"Brady," Alyssa said in a thin voice. She stepped right up to him and slipped her small hands into both of his. "Marco's mom called us a couple hours ago." She traded glances with Marco, who cupped the nape of her neck and squeezed.

"Aw, shit, man. Is it your dad?" Brady asked. Dread filled his chest like black ink. Nick Vieri was a damn good man and stepped in willingly and unconditionally to help him and Alyssa, especially Alyssa.

Marco's lips pressed into a tight line as he shook his head.

Brady frowned. "Well, then—"

"It's ours," Alyssa said.

"What?" A hum, like white noise on speed, buzzed in Brady's ears.

Tears pooled in Aly's red-rimmed eyes. "They're not sure when it happened, but—"

He tugged his hands free and retreated a step. His heart rate took off at a sprint. "When *what* happened?"

Alyssa reached for his hand, but Brady yanked it away. He needed to hear the words. He needed her to *say* the words. "Dad…died," she said, her voice cracking.

"No." Brady shook his head. "*No*."

"They're doing an autopsy to determine—"

"*No*," he roared. "That fucking son of a bitch!"

Tears dropped down Alyssa's cheeks. "I know—"

"No you fucking don't!" *Aw, Jesus. Aw, God. It was all ruined now.*

Marco stepped in front of Alyssa and placed a hand on Brady's chest. "Brady—"

His skin was so tight, the contact was like being electrocuted. His sight went red and he shoved Marco's arm away, clipping him in the face. Marco stumbled. Alyssa screamed. Marco shouted…words he couldn't make out.

Brady's headed pounded. *Now he couldn't… Now he would never be able to…* He crashed into something, into Marco. *Fucking son of a bitch would even die to hurt me.*

Arm twisted behind his back, his face met the wall. A deep throb set into his cheekbone.

"Brady! *Dammit, Brady*!" Marco's voice was sharp as steel and sliced through the fog in Brady's brain.

"Get off me," he rasped. "Get the fuck off me."

Marco released him and stepped back, eyes wary, shoulders tense. Blood oozed from his busted bottom lip.

Breathing hard, Brady fell back against the wall and braced his hands on his knees. He wrestled the frenzied emotion back into a box and locked it tight. The extrication felt like a surgery that hadn't healed. That never would. He used the raw ache to center himself.

Finally, he raised his gaze to Marco, whose eyes held no reproach, no censure, only an understanding born of a lifetime of being on the front lines of Brady's life. Marco nodded and his body relaxed.

"Fuck," Brady bit out, the flash fire of his fight extinguished. He glanced around. Aly was gone. *Oh, God, Alyssa.*

Marco's big hand landed on his shoulder. "She's fine. She's in the car. You have to know she knows you well enough to expect you to take it bad. It's why we're here. Why she didn't just call."

Brady scrubbed his hands over his head and mentally battened down all his emotional hatches. Tight again, he let it all just roll off, just roll the fuck off. Just like always. "How is she?"

Marco shrugged. "Sad. Pissed. Relieved. The whole gamut. She's tough, though. She'll be okay."

"Yeah." Brady blew out a breath. "I should apologize to her. She doesn't need this shit."

Marco nodded and led the way onto the front porch. Brady stepped out behind him. His gaze settled on Alyssa, leaning against the hood of Betty, Marco's affectionate name for the black '67 Mustang his grandfather had left him years ago.

The moment she saw him, she was in motion. Alyssa hit his chest running full force, and Brady caught and held her tight.

"I'm sorry I'm such a hothead," he rasped against her hair. "I'm just like him."

She gasped and yanked back. "No. No, you're not. Don't you ever say that again."

"Okay," he said. "Okay." He stroked her dark hair.

She buried her face against him and the tears poured out of her, wetting his T-shirt and soaking through to his skin. He would bear it. He would bear anything for his sister. She was the only thing he'd ever done right.

He looked up at Marco, standing with his arms crossed, his expression tight, and his eyes on Alyssa.

Brady kissed Aly's hair. "Shit, what a pair we are, huh?"

Alyssa sobbed-laughed. "Yeah."

He pulled back and cupped her face, his thumbs catching her tears, wiping them away. "We're okay, Aly. You know? It's over," he said, giving her the words she needed to hear. "It's over now. And you have a clean slate."

She nodded, more tears falling.

He caught those, too. "Yeah?"

"Yeah." She heaved a shuddering breath and fisted her tears away. Alyssa's stomach growled, then growled again.

Brady cocked an eyebrow, earning a small smile from his sister.

She shrugged. "We came here as soon as we got off the phone, so we haven't eaten."

"You want something? We could order Chinese." Brady glanced between Alyssa and Marco.

"Sure," she said.

Marco nodded. "I could eat."

"Okay," Brady said, arm around his sister's shoulders. "Let's get some food and figure out what we have to do next."

Chapter Twelve

Joss got home late Wednesday night after having dinner with Christina. She'd promised to fill her in on all the details from her doctor's appointment, so after work they went to their favorite Mexican restaurant and had their usuals — minus the margaritas.

Given what she'd eaten, Joss *really* hoped this wasn't a bad night for her stomach. She'd only had one other day as miserable as Friday, so clearly she wasn't going to escape having at least some morning sickness. Although, seriously, if that name wasn't some false advertising she didn't know what was.

She got out of her truck and made her way up the sidewalk, then hesitated. It was pushing ten o'clock, but the lights were still on at Brady's place. Anticipation of when she'd tell him and what she'd say and how he'd react had been driving her crazy all week. It wasn't like there was some perfect time to break this news, was it? The sooner she told him, the sooner she could stop worrying about it.

And Christina was right. Even if Brady was upset and refused to take any part in the baby's life, Joss would still have something she'd wanted forever—a family.

Right? Right. So… Okay.

She followed the sidewalk to Brady's front door. A herd of butterflies tore through her stomach.

Her fist shook when she raised it to knock.

Brady answered almost right away, beer bottle in hand. His brown eyes were flat as they stared at her. "Joss," he finally said.

"Hey. Um." *This is going great already. Maybe I should—*

"Did you want to come in?" he asked, turning away.

"Uh, sure." She stepped in behind him. "Wow. What a difference your new furniture makes." A rich brown leather sofa and chair nearly matched in color the two end tables and coffee table that filled the space. In the dining room sat a small rectangular table with two chairs.

"Yeah. I guess," Brady said and held up his beer. "Want one?"

"Oh. No, thanks." He stared at her, his face so…expressionless. Something was wrong. "Is everything okay, Brady?"

He set the bottle down and chuffed out a humorless laugh. "Couldn't be better."

"You know what? I'll come back—"

His expression shifted. For a moment, she would've sworn he was terrified. His eyes went wide and wild. A tingle of *oh shit* fluttered through her stomach.

He stepped right into her space and cupped his hands around the back of her head. "It's all ruined now," he rasped.

"What is?" She curled her fingers around his wrists,

needing to hold him back, even though she knew she should stay away. He was dangerous to her heart, her ego. And he didn't know...

"Everything." Heat and need slipped into his gaze, though it didn't replace the wildness. The look promised to devour her. Despite herself, Joss's body responded, her nipples peaking inside her clothing.

Suddenly, they were kissing. She didn't know if he'd leaned down or she'd pushed up. Their tongues twirled and fought. Their hands squeezed and tugged. Their bodies pressed and rubbed.

And none of it was enough.

He pushed her back one step, another, until her spine encountered the wall beside the front door.

Joss was instantly wet, even as the certainty coursed through her that this was a bad idea, a bad way to resolve whatever was troubling Brady so deeply. But another part of her yearned to comfort him, to help him forget, to give him a hand over whatever yawning emotional gorge he was staring down, even if for only a short while. Stupid, given what he'd done the last time she'd entertained such feelings. But she hadn't yet been able to resist him.

And now that she carried his baby, it was harder than ever.

"I need you," Brady rasped against her lips. Joss nodded. "I'm sorry—"

"Talk later," she murmured.

Hands fumbled at buttons and zippers. He tugged her shirt up and her pants and panties down. They pooled at her ankles. She kicked her heels off and her clothes away as he shoved his jeans and boxers to his knees.

Breathing hard, he kissed one eye, then the other, then her nose, then the corner of her mouth. The adoration warmed every cold place inside her. His fingers slipped between her legs, teasing, stroking, spreading her slickness. "Turn around, Joss."

A hot thrill shot through her. She turned her back to him and braced her hands on the wall.

Brady gripped her hips and pulled, forcing her to bend over. And then he was in her, filling her, stretching her. Joss cried out at the erotic invasion.

"Jesus," he growled. "More amazing every fucking time."

He started moving then, a slow pace that had him trembling. Joss got the distinct impression he was struggling to hold himself back, to control how much he needed this, needed her.

"Let go, Brady. Just let yourself go. I can handle it. I've got you."

His fingers dug into the flesh of her hips. "Joss," he rasped.

"Let go."

He did.

Brady hammered into her so hard she had to spread her feet to steady herself. The sound of his hips slapping against her cheeks filled the room. The frenzied pace set her body immediately on edge and held her there until the sensation was deliciously painful.

And then he wrapped himself around her. One hand gripping a breast and the other her shoulder, he hunched himself over her body and came at her with a series of quick, deep strokes she felt everywhere.

A single moment of imagining what they must look like with his big body curled around hers so possessively had energy barreling through Joss's center, making her wetter, shoving her closer to a shattering orgasm.

The room was filled with their soundtrack—his rough, panting breaths punctuated by occasional groans, her higher-pitched moans and whimpers, the wet sound of their bodies crashing together over and over. The way he was all over her made her feel claimed down to her very soul. Even though this was rough and fast and dirty, Joss felt that something important was passing between them. Something far more intense than the last time they'd been together.

His need felt like a tangible presence in the room.

Brady's hand slipped from her breast and settled between her legs. His fingers flicked over her clit in time with his deep, hard thrusts.

Out of nowhere, Joss's orgasm slammed into her. She cried out and wrapped an arm around his bicep, afraid she was going to fall.

"Fuck," he bit out. Holding her so tight now she struggled to breathe, Brady came, his hips still moving in halting strokes as he poured himself into her. His harsh breaths feathered over her shoulder. For long minutes after their bodies were spent, they remained in the same position.

His head thudded against her shoulder.

She reached back and dragged her fingers through his hair, and he nuzzled into her neck, dropped kisses behind her ear. His arms wrapped around her so tightly, she wasn't sure if he was embracing her or holding on for dear life. "Joss," he whispered, his breath caressing her skin.

Her heart raced as much from hope as the physical exertion she'd just experienced.

This time felt different. This time he wasn't pulling away.

The thought gave her the courage to say what she'd come over here for in the first place.

"Brady?" She rubbed his arms.

"Yeah?" He kissed her shoulder and pulled away. Thoughtfully, he handed her his clothes and then put his back together.

Joss watched him as she redressed. He appeared as shaky as she felt, like the sex, the connection, had affected him as deeply.

"I need to tell you something, okay?"

He nodded and reached for her, his arms wrapping around her shoulders, pulling her in close. He kissed her hair.

Her heart squeezed, and she took a deep breath. Now or never. "Okay." The words sat on the tip of her tongue, hung there. She tried to shove them out, but they wouldn't budge.

Brady pulled back enough to meet her eyes. Such anguish. "What is it?"

"I'm pregnant."

His eyes went wide and he shook his head. "You're *what*?" he bit out, his voice full of disbelief.

Cracks snaked across the surface of her joyful hope. "Pregnant. I—"

His eyes narrowed to ice-cold slits as he stepped away. A storm rolled in across his features. "You've *got* to be fucking kidding me." His nostrils flared, and his hands fisted.

The cracks grew wider, more numerous, weakening the very ground beneath her feet. Dizziness threatened to swamp her.

Oh, God. His words made it hard to breathe. He'd never talked to her like that before. Her muscles ached from the effort to stand her ground, hold onto her shattering hope.

"Brady—"

"You told me you were on birth control."

The accusation came through loud and clear, making her stomach toss, making it obvious he didn't care—not about her or the baby. "I *am* on birth control. I don't know how this happened. I just know that it has."

He grabbed the beer off the table. "How do you know it's mine?"

Her head swam, her hope in a flat-out free fall now. "*What?* I can't believe you just said that."

A furious red climbed up his face. "Why the hell wouldn't I? If you'd have a one-night stand with me, what's to say there haven't been others?"

The room's walls buckled and went wavy. She clutched at the nearest one for support. "I told you the truth about my history," she said, her throat tight, eyes stinging. "I hadn't been with anyone for over six months before you. And there's been no one since."

He scoffed and muttered under his breath, then took a long pull from the beer bottle.

Asshole. "I can't believe—"

"What exactly is it you want from me?"

Joss shook her head and retreated a full step, her arm coming around her stomach. "Want? I don't *want* anything. *God.* You know, I didn't expect you to be thrilled about this, but I didn't think you'd be such a prick about it, either."

He held out his arms. "I am what I am. Regretting me yet?"

Rage and hurt flooded through her veins in equally scorching amounts. She turned and walked out the door.

A crash sounded from behind her, but no freaking way was Joss going back to see what it was. If she never saw Brady

Scott again, it would be too soon.

Anger tugged at every muscle in her body until she thought she'd snap in two. It flowed through her, demanding release, but there was nothing, *nothing* she could do to vent the horrible, suffocating mass of it. Even worse, her house's proximity to Brady's made it impossible to give voice to one note of her pain. She refused to chance giving him the satisfaction of hearing how his words had torn her apart.

His rejection of her was one thing—she'd been discarded so many times she was now a pro at it. But to reject this child? This completely innocent and defenseless being growing inside her?

No. *No*.

Her son or daughter would *never* taste even a single crumb of the rejection and abandonment Joss had swallowed by the mouthful her whole life.

Over my dead body.

She paced around her house until she thought she might go crazy. She wanted to go somewhere. Anywhere. Despite the hour, she picked up her phone and dialed.

"Hey," Christina answered.

"Hi," Joss rasped, restrained tears making her voice waver.

"Oh, no." Christina knew from their conversation over dinner that she was considering telling Brady tonight.

"Yeah."

"*Bastard*. I'm coming over."

Joss shook her head, swallowed hard. "No. I was wondering…could I—"

"Yes. Come any time. My spare bedroom is your spare bedroom. Are you sure you can drive?"

She batted away a runaway tear. "Yeah. You don't think

Tony will mind?"

"Tony loves you. You know that. He'll be glad to see you."

"Okay. Thank you."

"Joss, drive safe."

"I will. See you soon."

When they disconnected, Joss was in motion. She packed two days' worth of work clothes and a set of pajamas. Panties, toiletries, brushes, and makeup went into her bag next. She grabbed her favorite pillow off her bed, and then, downstairs, she gathered her purse and keys.

She threw everything into her truck and tore out of the lot before she chanced even a spare look in the direction of Brady's house.

The farther away she got from him, the more she could breathe.

• • •

Thick stands of trees and farm fields heavy with overripe corn flashed by as Brady made his way up Interstate 270 to Frederick, the town where he'd been born and grown up. The town where his bastard of a father now lay cold and dead in a metal drawer.

Ahead of him, Marco and Alyssa rode in Betty. Brady had met them at their new apartment first thing that morning, but they'd agreed to take separate cars so it would be easier to accomplish the various tasks the next few days might entail.

The only problem was that his solitude left him no reprieve from the memory of the horrible way he'd treated

Joss.

Pregnant.

Jesus Christ.

When the word had first fallen from between her soft pink lips, Brady couldn't believe his ears. No way the universe would be so capricious, so twisted, so cruel as to give him the very thing he could never let himself have on the very day he learned once and for all he couldn't have it.

Confronting his father, unleashing the words he'd buried deep down inside himself, seeing the old man's expressions as Brady made him understand everything his actions had wrought—these were supposed to be his way up…out… through… He didn't even know the right way to describe it. Just *free*. Free of the hate and the anger and the pain he'd slogged through these past ten years.

But, no, Brady hadn't heard wrong.

After the words sank in, agonizing rage petrified every part of his brain save the portion responsible for his fight-or-flight response. And fight he had. He'd flung one emotional grenade after another until the only woman he'd ever cared for—ever wanted—was bruised and battered and bloodied.

And yet she'd stood.

Brady's heart squeezed in his chest. For a long moment, he struggled to breathe.

She'd stood up for herself. For her child.

Their child.

His child.

My child.

The very thought flushed shards of ice through his veins and shredded his insides with fear. The one thing he knew— the *only* thing he knew—was that no child deserved to grow up in a house filled with anger and anguish. And right now, Brady was drowning in them. And he couldn't see clear to the shore.

Up shit's creek without a paddle.

He nodded to himself. That about summed it up.

Finally, their caravan arrived at Marco's parents' house. They lived in a red brick colonial on the other side of the neighborhood from where Brady and Alyssa had lived. He felt the presence of their childhood home like a fog hanging heavy in the air, chilling and disquieting. Some time in these next few days they were going to have to face it.

When he rounded the back of his truck, Alyssa was walking down the driveway. She came to him and wrapped him in her arms. He returned the embrace.

"What's this for?" he asked.

"Because we both need it."

He squeezed her for one last moment and then led them to the house.

Nick Vieri was out the front door before they'd made it up the sidewalk. Tall and dark, one look at him and you could never deny he and Marco were related. "Brady, Alyssa." He hugged Aly tight and whispered words of condolence. Brady extended his hand. Nick accepted it and pulled him in for a hug, as well. "I'm sorry about your loss, son," he said.

Brady stepped back. "It occurred years ago."

"Yes," the older man said, his bright blue eyes sympathetic and kind. "Come on in. Do you have bags I can help with?"

Brady grinned. "Marco can get them." A hand smacked the back of his head. Brady spun on his heel to find Marco glaring at him. "What was that for?"

"Your lazy ass can help me."

Alyssa rolled her eyes. "Are you two twelve?"

"Pretty much," Brady said.

"Sometimes," Marco said at almost the same time. He tugged her into him, making her laugh.

Inside, the house smelled amazing, like garlic and fresh, warm bread. They made their way into the kitchen and found Lily Vieri setting the table with a feast for twenty. She'd always had a knack for making anyone feel right at home. She turned and smiled. "Hi, kids."

One by one, she gave the three of them hugs and kisses, ending with Marco. She rubbed his forearm, the one heavily scarred from an explosion and multiple surgeries. "How are you feeling?"

Marco's expression was soft as he looked down at his mom. "Better and better."

She squeezed his hand and pulled him farther into the kitchen.

The five of them sat down to a feast of homemade lasagna, garden salad, and garlic bread. It was the best meal he'd had in months—except for Joss's waffles. He shoved the thought away and allowed nostalgia to curl around his shoulders as he thought of all the meals he'd enjoyed at this table over the years. Even before his mom died, he was a regular fixture at the Vieris'. Afterward, well, this house had become more than a home away from home. It had become a safe haven.

As everyone finished their meals, the conversation turned to the situation that had brought them all together again.

Nick leaned back in his chair. "So, how can we help? What part of this can we take off your shoulders?"

Brady looked between Nick and Lily, and then to Alyssa. "Alyssa and I talked yesterday. Neither of us wants the house."

"I have a good friend who is a Realtor. I'll be happy to call her," Lily said.

Brady nodded. "We…I guess…" He met Alyssa's gaze. "We'll go through it, first. See if there's anything we want." He had no desire to step foot in the place, but he knew Aly was hoping some of their mom's belongings might still be in the house. Doubtful, but worth the look, for her. "The rest can be donated or thrown away."

Lily nodded. "She can arrange for the place to be cleaned out. We can handle those details."

"Thank you," Brady and Alyssa both said.

Alyssa rested her forearms on the table. "We have an appointment first thing in the morning to go to the funeral home. We know he already has a burial plot next to our mother. But as far as holding a service or a viewing or anything, do you think anyone would come?"

"People will come for the two of you," Nick said.

Brady's gaze dropped to the table. The air sucked out of the room, and he felt like he was about to crawl out of his skin and had to get out from under everyone's eyes to do it. "This was delicious as usual, Lily." He rose from the table. "I'll grab our things from the cars." Without waiting for a response, Brady excused himself from the table and bolted for the front door.

He walked around the far side of his Land Rover until he was shielded from the view of the house, and fell heavily back against the quarter panel. The kindness and compassion the Vieris extended felt undeserved with the guilt over the way he'd treated Joss weighing on him so heavily.

Footsteps approached from the driveway. Brady heaved

a deep breath and crossed his arms.

Nick rounded the back of the truck and fell into place beside Brady. Marco had inherited his quiet intensity from this man, so Brady knew he was working his way toward saying something.

Finally, he spoke. "This is going to be harder for you than for Alyssa, yes?"

Frowning, Brady turned his gaze to the older man.

"She's grieved many times before now, but you never have."

"What is there to grieve?" Brady said, defensiveness rising like high tide within him.

Nick's blue eyes were piercing. "Lie to Alyssa if you must, son, but don't lie to yourself."

Brady turned away.

Nick pushed off the truck and clapped Brady on the shoulder. "Why don't we get the house over with this afternoon? You three can ride in your truck and I'll drive mine. That'll give us enough cargo space in case there are things you and Alyssa want to bring home."

Brady met his gaze and nodded, trying like hell to prevent even a whisper of his anxiety from shining back at the other man. "Yeah."

Brady, Alyssa, and Marco rode in silence the four blocks to the Scott house. He parked his Rover at the curb and glared at the rancher like it was his mortal enemy.

He schooled his expression before turning to Alyssa. "Ready?"

Her gaze surveyed the front of the house. "Yeah. Let's get this done."

Empty cardboard boxes in hand, Nick met them on the lawn, if that's what you could call the overgrown jungle that was the front of the place. Brady flipped around the keys on his ring until he singled out a beat-up silver key he usually just ignored. He hadn't used it in nearly a decade. Maybe it wouldn't even work anymore.

No such luck.

Brady pushed open the door, hesitated for the length of a breath, and stepped inside.

Hot, stale, smoky air choked the inside of the house, which was as run-down on the interior as it was on the exterior. The walls were yellowed and the paint peeling, the couch cushions were annihilated from overuse, and the floors probably hadn't seen a vacuum cleaner since Brady moved out. "Jesus," he said under his breath.

Alyssa slapped her hand over her mouth and nose. "How did he live in this?"

"I'll open some windows," Marco said, squeezing her shoulder. It wasn't as easy a task as he thought since he had to fight against a decade's worth of disuse. Some took convincing to open, while others wouldn't budge.

"I want to look in my room," Aly said. She and Marco disappeared through the living room arch and down the hall.

Brady was rooted in place, his stomach sour, his chest tight. The absolute squalor of the conditions before him coursed twin reactions through his veins: guilt that their father had lived like this for so many years, and dark satisfaction at the justice of it all.

"Joseph was a very sick man," Nick said.

The comment pulled Brady out of his thoughts. He nodded. "I'll go check on Alyssa."

Down the hall, the air was older, stiller, thicker. He passed his parents' closed bedroom door and stopped. He held the knob for a long moment and finally pushed.

The bed was made. Thick layers of dust covered every surface, but otherwise the room was…pristine. Just as he remembered it. From before. "Hey, Al?"

"Yeah?" she called. She came up next to him. "Oh, my God."

She and Brady walked into the room, and Nick and Marco gathered at the door.

"It's like he never came in here," she said. The truth of her observation hung as heavy in the air as the dust they'd disturbed. Alyssa crossed to the long dresser. "All her stuff is still here," she said, her voice no more than a whisper.

Brady was at her side in an instant. The silver brush and hand mirror set she prized but never used. The rectangular tray filled with perfume bottles of every size, shape, and color. Her lacquered jewelry box with the tiny dancing ballerina hidden away inside. Alyssa lifted the lid.

The blue velvet was bright and unblemished, the top having protected the inside from the passage of time.

"Nick, can we get a few boxes in here?" Brady asked. When he turned around, three empties were lined up on the bed. "You take anything you want, Aly. Even if you're not sure, you take it."

She nodded and lifted the jewelry box into her hands, leaving behind a ghostly impression where it had sat all these years. Seeing Alyssa's heavy-hearted joy at the preservation of some of their mom's things forced Brady to acknowledge a grudging feeling of appreciation toward their father. It was the least—literally—he could've done for Aly, after everything.

Alyssa scoured the room and the closets and packed

what she wanted into boxes. "What's up there?" she asked.

Brady followed her gaze to the closet's ceiling, where molding outlined a pull-down door to the attic. He tugged the hanging string, forcing the stairs to fold out with an angry screech. "I'll go up."

He flipped the switch on the wall by the stairs' opening, but the light didn't work. In fact, now that he thought about it, there was no electrical hum anywhere in the house. He opened the flashlight app on his phone and shone it around the space. "Come on up and bring some boxes, just in case."

Alyssa and Marco climbed the creaky stairs and used the lights on their phones to look around.

Boxes of books and clothes they sat aside right away. Boxes of photographs or albums they handed down to Nick, who hung out at the ready on the stairs for just that purpose.

"Oh, look," Alyssa said. She held up a set of baby clothes and matching shoes. "Look how small you were."

Brady ground his teeth together, the irony of her discovery a kick in the gut. "How do you know they were mine and not yours?"

She smiled. "Because it says, 'God loves little boys.'"

He grunted and turned away as Alyssa handed the box to Nick.

Brady worked through one stack of boxes, then another. On a shelf behind a third stack, he found a long rectangular box with a faded floral design outlining each corner of the cover. The lid stuck, but finally Brady nudged it free.

Peeling away layers of folded tissue revealed fabric. Brady scanned his flashlight over the contents, and finally they made sense. *Holy shit.* This had to be their mom's.

"Aly, come here. I have something for you."

She stepped around the boxes and made her way to him. "What did you find?"

Keeping his light on the box for her, he moved out of the way so she could get in closer.

Her gasp hit him right in the solar plexus. She reached out but stopped just short of touching the beadwork that sparkled down the front.

"What is it?" Marco asked.

"It's…I think it must be my mother's wedding dress."

Brady met Marco's gaze and nodded, then moved away from the corner so the two of them could have a moment. Soft whispers ended abruptly when Alyssa burst into tears. The sound crawled down Brady's spine, awakening every protective instinct he'd ever had. But there was no need. Marco had Alyssa wrapped tightly within his embrace.

Out of nowhere, loneliness and jealousy slammed into him. As he watched them love and comfort one another, Brady's heart ached and his stomach sank. Would he ever have that?

Probably not.

And certainly not with the woman he wanted. Not after yesterday.

He made for the stairs and descended, unable to meet Nick's gaze. A few moments later, Alyssa and Marco joined them. Her eyes were glassy. Brady met her gaze and silently asked if she was okay. She gave him a single nod.

Seeing her emotion, Brady suddenly realized how *little* he felt. Maybe the house didn't hold the ghosts he'd feared. Maybe the sad state of the place removed all the power it had once held. He didn't know the why of it, just that, standing there in the middle of the childhood home he'd dreaded returning to, he felt a whole lot of nothing.

Chapter Thirteen

The next two days passed in a blur. The visit to the funeral home. The meeting with the Realtor. The friggin' shopping trip to the mall to buy their dad a suit in which to be buried. The call from the coroner's office informing them Joseph Scott had died of cancers of the lung and liver. No surprise there.

It turned out both Alyssa and Nick were right—the single closed-casket viewing they'd decided to host was very poorly attended, but the nine people who did stop in to pay their respects were all there for them: Brady's high school baseball coach, three of Marco and Alyssa's former colleagues from Whiskey's Music Roadhouse, Marco's long-time friend Max who owned a gym in town, a couple of high school friends.

Through it all, Brady felt like he was underwater—sounds seemed muffled, sensations felt dulled, movement took astounding effort. Everything was distant. In spare moments, he found himself thinking of Joss, wanting to see her, considering slipping next door and into her arms. And then he'd remember where he was. What he was doing. And that he'd fucked up anything he might've tried to build with Joss Daniels. The pain sucker-punched him anew every time.

Sunday morning dawned bright and sunny. A beautiful September day. He came down to breakfast to find Marco and Alyssa huddled around some photo albums on the table. One whiff of stale air told him they were from his parents' house.

"Oh, my God, Brady. You have to see these," Alyssa said, smiling up at him.

Biting back his annoyance, he glanced down. Baby pictures. Lying down. Propped up. In a bathtub.

He turned the page. More of the same. He flipped again, and frowned.

Brady turned back to the beginning of the album. His mother had written his name and birth date on the first page. What was it that had caught his attention? He studied each of the pictures more carefully this time.

Some of them were of the baby alone, but the rest were of Brady and his mom…which meant his dad had taken the pictures.

He tried to imagine those moments. His dad, carrying a camera around, trigger-happy and proud enough to capture every single ordinary moment of Brady's new life for posterity.

My *father did this?*

In one photograph where Brady had been old enough to sit up, he held a baseball glove in his lap as he mouthed a baseball. A wooden bat sat on the floor next to him.

The longer he stared at the image, the more his brain swam.

"Man, I didn't remember that at all," Marco said.

Brady dragged his gaze from the baby picture. "What?"

Marco turned the photo album around and tapped his finger against the edge of a team picture. Brady leaned in. It was one of their early peewee baseball teams. He scanned the players and easily found himself and Marco, standing together in the back row. "What don't you remember?"

"Look again."

Brady stared.

"Look at the *coaches*," Marco finally said.

For a moment, Brady's heart stopped, and then tripped over itself to start again. His father stood at the far end of the row in a team jersey. He pulled the book out of Marco's hand, studied the team picture, then flipped through the pages.

No. No freaking way. This was *not* his father. His father had never cared about him, about either of them. He sure as shit wasn't the kind of guy who coached his kid's baseball team.

Except… It was right there in faded Kodak color. But then why was the story these images told so totally foreign to him? It was like spying on strangers, or some shadow family where the people looked familiar but their happiness was an alternate universe.

The strangest sense of vertigo gripped him until he had to grasp the edge of the table.

How could I not remember?

For the second time in as many weeks, the past showed up like Dickens's ghosts to reveal something he'd believed to the marrow of his bones wasn't exactly as it seemed.

When his head stopped swimming, Brady excused himself from the table and went upstairs to shower and dress for the funeral.

Twenty minutes later he stood in front of the bathroom mirror in his Class As. When he ensured everything was squared away, he grabbed his green beret and went downstairs. He found Nick and Lily in the living room, but the others were still upstairs. The men nodded at each other and Lily fussed over Brady's uniform, then he took up a position at the front window, stewing, seething, a human volcano.

Goddammit. Those pictures were burrowing deep and insidiously under his skin, making it hard to cling to his rage, making him feel like a fucking idiot for not remembering. How the hell could he not remember what life had been like *before*? And what did that mean *now*? No way was he forgiving his bastard of a father. Not after everything. He couldn't.

If he did, if he let go of the anger, he'd have nothing left.

A few moments later, Marco and Alyssa came downstairs. Brady mentally secured all his shit and turned to find them hand-in-hand. He had to fight off the fleeting wish that Joss was with him right now, her hand in his, skin to skin. She would be compassionate and kind, like the day she'd taken care of him, but sarcastic, too, keeping him laughing when he needed the lift.

The deep need for companionship—no, for *her* companionship—threatened to yank the floor right out from under his spit-shined dress shoes.

Enough.

They made a sad, two-car procession to the graveside service. Brady got out and met the others on the far side of the car. The minute he laid eyes on the casket centered over the yawning hole in the ground, every bit of sensation he hadn't been able to feel the past two and a half days slammed back into him.

Somehow, he made it to the row of fabric-covered chairs that lined the site. White-hot agony crawled up his spine and through his gut. He felt rubbed raw, like his skin no longer protected his nervous system. He didn't hear a word anyone said.

He couldn't breathe.

Alyssa tugged on his sleeve. He flinched and turned to find everyone getting up, Marco's parents shaking the offici-ant's hand.

His sister stepped to the spray of red roses atop the cas-ket and pulled a long stem free. She brought it to her lips, kissed it, and laid it atop the gleaming wood.

The trembling made his teeth ache. His sight went hazy red. And he clenched his fists so hard he thought he might snap his knuckles.

He glared hatred and contempt at the casket and hoped his father's bones shriveled to dust under the force of it.

Joseph Scott had stolen *everything*.

He'd stolen Alyssa's entire teenage years. Denied her their only remaining parent.

His actions had obliterated the memories of the parts of Brady's childhood that were good.

He'd stolen the carefree senior year Brady should've had. Any chance at college.

His sense of safety. His sense of belonging. His sense of self-worth.

Joss.

Joss and my baby.

Brady slammed his fists down on top of the casket, once, twice.

Arms banded around his chest. Hauled him back. Voices shouted.

"I've lost her. I've lost her and it's your fault. Do you hear me? It's your fucking fault!"

"Brady. Brady, stop. Come on, son. Talk to me."

Soul-deep mourning erupted on the heels of the anger. He grieved for his mother, for Alyssa, for himself, for his father—yes, even for his father, who had been no more than a dead man walking for ten long years.

And, oh God, the grief he felt over Joss and the baby…

"She'll never forgive me," Brady rasped, grabbing his chest.

A big hand curled around his cheek. "Son, who are you talking about?"

The question pulled Brady out of his private vigil. His eyes came into focus on Nick's face, the man's expression tight with concern and sympathy. It was all too much. He *felt* too much. He *hurt* too much. Brady jerked out of Marco's hold and paced between the flat grave markers, the world vibrating around him.

"Brady, talk to us. Let us help."

He whirled and stalked up to his best friend. He pointed at Marco's left arm, the scars mostly hidden by the dark gray suit he wore. "*That*…that should've been me. My whole life, you've been the truest friend I've ever had. And you didn't deserve that. But I—"

Marco's good fist cracked into Brady's jaw and jarred his head so hard his ears rang. Brady staggered and just managed to keep himself on his feet.

"Marco!" Nick yelled.

Brady backhanded the blood from the corner of his mouth. The fog, the haze, the rising tide of rage—they faded away. "Dude. What the *hell* was that for?"

"Don't you ever, *ever* say that again," Marco said in a tight, seething voice. "Most of the time, I m-manage to accept that I didn't de-de—" He clenched his eyes tight. It was the worst Brady had ever seen his injury-born apraxia trouble him, but Marco heaved a breath, opened his eyes again, and nailed Brady with a glare. "But you didn't d-deserve it either. You haven't deserved any of this shit." He waved a hand at the casket, then tugged it roughly through his hair and turned away.

He whipped back in his face a moment later. "Jesus Christ, Brady. You think I don't know what you think of y-yourself? All these years, you don't think I've noticed you've never had anything more than a one-night stand or a fuck buddy? You don't think I realize that the way you keep a lid on the boiling cauldron in your head is by beating yourself the fuck up?" He glared at Brady a long minute. "That's why I hit you, by the way. 'Cause I'm just fucked up enough to give you what you need. Feeling a little better?"

Brady stared at him, but could see by the expression on Marco's face he knew the answer. And damn if he wasn't right. After that punch, Brady's head was clearer than it had been in days. Even though it hurt like a mofo.

"I will help you six ways from Sunday, but, man, seriously, you *have* to find a way to let go of the anger. I'm not saying you didn't come by that shit honestly. You did. But it is eating you from the inside out. And I hate that. I hate that for you. I hate that for Aly."

Brady gestured toward the grave. "He was supposed to be my way to let go. I was supposed to… And then the fucker up and died. And now…" He shook his head, at a loss for words, at a loss for so many things.

Nick stepped next to Marco. "He wouldn't have given you what you needed, Brady. He never could. And you never needed him to."

Brady glanced between the Vieri men. "But…but then… Aw, *hell*." His father had inadvertently given him the only things he could. Proof that, once, the man had been capable of love. Proof that Brady could choose which set of Joseph Scott's footsteps he wanted to follow. It was all on him, wasn't it?

And so far he was choosing so poorly it was almost laughable. Or it would've been if he weren't destroying himself and the people he loved, too.

Loved?

Did he love Joss?

He blew out a long breath and looked at Nick. His shoulders sagged. "I met someone. We've been on and off the past month or so. She told me the day before we came here she's pregnant." The relief of the admission made it easier to breathe.

Nick's eyes went wide.

"Wait," Marco said. "We were at your house for four hours that day."

Brady nodded. "She came over about an hour after you left."

"Oh. *Oh*. Oh, shit," he said.

"Right."

"So, not long after you learned of Joseph's death, she told you you were going to be a father?" Nick asked. Brady nodded, but couldn't meet his gaze. "And you didn't react well?"

Brady chuffed out a humorless laugh. "She called me a prick, and she was right."

"I like her already," Marco said. "Wait, this isn't…is this your neighbor, uh, uh…"

"Joss. Yeah."

"I knew it," Marco said, the hint of a grin playing around his lips.

Brady rolled his eyes. "Yeah, yeah, Einstein. Whatever."

Nick stepped in front of Brady, his expression as serious as he'd ever seen it. "You've lost your mother and father, Brady. But, this woman? Do you love her?"

"I don't even know what that—"

"Bullshit," Nick said, his bright blue eyes intense and inescapable. "You love Alyssa as fiercely as any brother ever has, and you always have. You know what love is."

Brady stared at the man a long moment. Emotion welled within him, tightening his chest, kick-starting his heart.

If he could let go of the anger, he *would* have something left after all, wouldn't he? Joss could be there. And their child. But only if he did some serious manning up. And that started with being honest, with Nick, with himself.

"Maybe. Probably." He swallowed, hard. "Yes."

• • •

Joss knew the knock would come. Once she left her little refuge at Christina's, she knew it would. But as she lay in bed reading a book at ten thirty Sunday night, she still found herself unprepared for it.

She debated not answering, but when it continued, she decided there was no use in avoiding this conversation. Whether it was tonight, tomorrow, or next week, she knew down to her toes she'd have to face it sometime.

She slipped on her fluffy pink robe, cinched the belt around her waist, and padded downstairs. Taking a deep breath, she opened the door.

Brady's big body filled the rectangular space of the doorway, and he stood before her in full dress uniform. Rows of ribbons and badges decorated the space over his heart. The beret he wore bore an orange shield with a sword atop crossed arrows. She soaked him in from head to toe before meeting his gaze. *God*, he was so freaking gorgeous. Even if he'd broken her heart.

There was a depth in his brown eyes she didn't remember seeing before. Or maybe that was just her emotions talking. She seemed to have more than her fair share, lately. "What's the occasion?" she finally asked. "Funeral."

Joss frowned and drew a breath to speak—

"Before you say anything," he continued, "may I please say something?"

She steeled herself. "Okay."

"May I come in?"

"No." She didn't have that much steel, not with her body reacting to the presence of his.

Brady pressed his lips into a line and nodded a single time. "I could not regret more the way I talked to you and the way I treated you. You didn't deserve it, not at all. And I know I reacted horribly to the news that you're…that you're pregnant. And if I could take it back, if I could do it over, I would. In a heartbeat."

She held up a hand, his words slinking around the outsides of her defenses. "Brady—"

"Please. Please let me finish."

She couldn't resist the earnest expression, the pleading eyes. She nodded.

"Thank you. It's just…I'm not good at this. At any of it. I've never done it before, and I—"

"Done what?"

His eyes blazed at her and he swallowed roughly. "Fallen in love."

She gasped and the room suddenly closed in. "You have to go." She grabbed the door and pushed it.

Brady blocked it with his arm. "Joss."

She stepped back. "No. I can't…you can't… Everything about you terrifies me, if you want to know the truth of it. Your temper. The hot and cold mood swings. Running every time things get too real. And I can't handle that, Brady. Not after the life I've led. I can't handle the fear, the uncertainty. I don't want to. I shouldn't have to. And I sure as *hell* will not subject my baby to it."

"Our baby."

"What?"

"You said 'my baby,' but he, or she, is mine, too."

Joss wrapped her arms around herself in an effort to hold it together, in an effort to stay in place. Because all she wanted to do was launch herself into his arms, bask in the warm promise of his words, and never let go.

Oh, God, he said he's fallen in love with me.

Instead, she shook her head and embraced the knife

slicing through her chest. "It doesn't matter. Not what you want. Not what I might wish I could have. None of that matters. The only thing that does is this baby's safety and well-being. He'll never think for a single, solitary moment that he wasn't wanted."

"But I do—"

"Go. Now. Please, just go." Grief choked her throat, made it hard to say the words.

"Joss—"

"Go. And, Brady, please. Make this easier on the both of us. Don't come visit. Don't talk to me. Okay? Let's just—" Tears pricked at her eyes.

Such a handsome, masculine face shouldn't bear such sadness, she thought as she watched him struggle with her requests.

"I'll go," he said in a low voice. "But I'm *here*. Do you hear me? All you have to do is knock, and I'll be here for you, Joss. All you have to do is knock."

Chapter Fourteen

Joss stood in the doorway to her small home office and stared at the mess. The bookshelf still lay in pieces on the floor. At first she'd left it because she planned to take Brady up on his offer of help. And then she'd felt too tired and sometimes sick to deal with it.

In the irony of all ironies, she needed to disassemble the pieces her blood and sweat had managed to get together in the first place. Now that her office needed to transition into a nursery, she no longer had room for it.

Down on her knees, Joss wrestled the half-constructed shelf into submission. An hour later she had the shelves stacked flat inside their boxes and all the dowels, screws, and nails back into their little plastic zipper bags. She shoved it all to the side of the room and reveled in the return of her workspace and of a floor she could walk on without breaking an ankle.

Staring around the small room, she imagined how she

might decorate it for the baby. She already knew she didn't want to know the sex, so that probably ruled out pink and blue. But maybe…yellow? Bright, warm, happy. Yeah, yellow would be the perfect color to welcome her son or daughter into the world.

"*Our baby,*" she heard Brady's voice say again.

"Thank you, conscience. Duly noted."

Two weeks had passed since she'd asked him to leave and not come back. And that's exactly what he'd done.

She couldn't deny that his words still tempted her. In fact, she believed he meant them into the very center of her being. But that didn't mean he would live by them when the going got tough. And if she gave him a chance, she would always wonder when he was going to blow up or walk out the door.

She just couldn't stomach the possibility.

After a quick shower, she ran to the store. Already her appetite had picked up—and she craved milkshakes like water. Chocolate, of course, made with vanilla ice cream and lots of chocolate syrup. And she was out of both. It was a crisis that couldn't be ignored a day longer.

When she got home, color drew her gaze immediately to her front door.

Flowers—pink roses—awaited her return.

Forgetting the bags of groceries for a moment, Joss approached the surprise gift like someone might jump out from behind it. There was no card, and…how odd. There were eight of them.

She lifted the vase and carried it in. Were they from Brady? And why eight?

She centered the arrangement on the dining room table

and gave the beautiful flowers a curious glance every time she passed them until, finally, their drooping faces and falling petals forced her to throw them away.

At least the mystery of the flowers helped pass the days until her doctor's appointment. She'd been anticipating it like crazy because she'd get to see the first picture of the baby.

On Friday afternoon, she took off work a little early to make the appointment. Christina came with her—a feat of scheduling they'd managed when Joss finally informed her director that she was pregnant and had her first ultrasound. Her boss agreed to cover Christina's position in the preschool room on the condition that Joss brought in the picture.

"You make that paper gown look *good*," Christina said as they waited for Dr. Charles.

"Shut up." Joss chuckled, the paper crinkling as she shifted. "Jus' sayin'."

"Uh-huh. Your time will come, my friend."

Christina grinned.

A knock sounded at the door and Dr. Charles entered. She was a beautiful woman with warm brown skin and long hair pulled back in a ponytail. "Hey, ladies. How are you?"

"Good," Joss said.

"How have you been feeling, Joss? Any morning sickness?" she asked as she washed her hands.

"Occasional, like two or three times a week, and usually at night."

"They should call it all-day sickness."

Joss smiled. "Right?"

They talked through some other questions for a few minutes while the doctor tugged the ultrasound machine closer to the examining table. Thank God Joss had been reading her pregnancy book so she knew to expect that this ultrasound involved a wand, a condom, and some lubrication, otherwise she might've been traumatized by how the doc needed to do it this time around.

Christina grimaced.

"Why are *you* grimacing? I'm the one the ultrasound machine is getting fresh with."

Christina smacked a hand over her mouth to hold in her laughter.

Dr. Charles grinned. "Go ahead and laugh. It's an important part of this whole process as far as I'm concerned. Do it as much as you can. Now…"

Joss turned her gaze to the monitor.

The doctor made some adjustments down below and then…

Joss gasped. "Is that—?"

"Your little peanut? Yes."

The doctor pointed out the head, the body, the beginnings of the arms. Peanut was a totally apt description, and Joss was immediately head over heels in love. She didn't even mind when her eyes filled with tears.

The doctor took some measurements. "Looks like you're at right about eight weeks and five days," she said. "This is predicting your due date at May 24th."

Eight weeks. Eight. *Eight.*

Goose bumps erupted across her skin. The flowers. She couldn't stop the whimper from spilling from her lips.

The doctor smiled. "Pretty cool seeing this for the first time, isn't it?"

Joss nodded. It was, it truly was. But she couldn't share the real reason she'd lost control of her emotions. It wasn't just the baby. It was that, apparently, Brady was paying enough attention to know just how far along she was.

That night as she lay in bed and tried to fall asleep, it took everything she had not to knock on the wall.

• • •

The gifts continued to arrive.

Brady had kept his word not to visit or talk to her, but she hadn't asked him not to leave her things, had she? *Such a pain in the ass.* The thought forced her to smile every time.

Usually, the gifts came on Saturdays, marking the weekly anniversary of their first time together.

The day after her ultrasound, she'd opened the door in the morning to find a handled bookstore bag sat between her interior and storm doors. She pulled out a popular pregnancy book she'd already bought for herself, but that fact didn't detract one bit from the thoughtfulness of the gift.

The following Saturday brought no front-door surprise. Not in the morning, nor in the afternoon. Joss buried herself in fund-raiser phone calls and e-mails to distract herself from the disappointment. By the end of the weekend, Joss had convinced herself she was glad for it—it bolstered her determination to stay away from the man who'd been slowly but surely weakening her resolve and tempting her heart.

That whole next week, the center was a madhouse of childhood excitement. Wednesday was Halloween, and everyone was looking forward to the annual costume parade they hosted at the end of the day. Parents took off from work early to cheer their kids on, and then they partied until the last kid went home. It was fun, but exhausting. An abundance of chocolate gave her a boost.

Joss drove home that night excited for trick-or-treating. Since she was a child, she'd always loved Halloween—it was the one day of the year you could pretend to be anything or anybody. And because the houses were so close together, Fairlington was prime trick-or-treating territory—she had dozens of kids to look forward to entertaining her all night long.

When she pulled into her space, her eyes were drawn immediately to her front door. There, amid the three carved pumpkins, cobwebbing she'd wound around the columns, and large skeleton she'd hung on her front door, sat a cardboard box.

She glanced at Brady's townhouse and pushed out of the truck.

Inside, she carried it to the kitchen counter and couldn't get the box open fast enough.

The picture on the plastic packaging made her grin as she ripped it open and unfolded the material within. She burst into laughter.

He'd sent her a baby Halloween costume—and not just any costume, either. He'd sent her an official US Army baby costume. It was made of a camouflaged fabric and the attached "helmet" and sleeves were lined with soft fleece. It had canvas detailing and a black army patch sewn on the front.

She hugged it to her chest and laughed until she cried. And then her tears were real. He was doing everything he could think of to show her he was in this, that he cared.

Was she really doing the right thing in excluding him from his child's life?

• • •

Brady had just plated some scrambled eggs when a knock sounded at the door. Sucking grease from his thumb, he made for the front of the house.

A princess, a pirate, and a cat stood on the other side. "Trick or treat!"

"Uh, oh, right. Halloween." *Oh, shit.* He had not prepared for this. What the hell was he going to do?

The pirate held out his sword. "Trick or treat or ye walk the plank, matey!"

Brady scrubbed his hand over his hair. "Well, you see. I didn't remember to get any candy."

The cat's lip trembled.

The pirate scowled.

"Okay, hold on, now." An idea came to mind. "Just wait here for a sec."

He ran upstairs to the coin jug he kept on the corner of his dresser. He grabbed a handful of money, uncertain what the going pirate ransom rate was these days. But the last thing he wanted was to be branded a Halloween cheapskate. He'd been a kid once. He remembered what happened to the houses that gave out health food or a single petrified Tootsie Roll. And he had his pride.

Back at the front door, he picked through the coins and dropped four quarters in each of the kids' buckets.

"Thanks, mister," the pirate said. The girls grinned. And then they all turned away.

Pleased with himself, Brady almost shut the door, but then he remembered the box he'd left on Joss's porch. Easing the screen door open again, he peered over the small garden that separated their porches. The box was gone. *Hell, yeah.*

He returned to his dinner with the warm weight of victory filling his chest. What would she think of the costume? Would it make her laugh? Would it make her talk to him?

He missed her like a thirst he couldn't quench. After his admission to Nick and Marco at the cemetery, his feelings gained a clarity he wasn't sure he'd ever before experienced. He wasn't deluded enough to think he had all his shit squared away—something his subsequent therapy appointments had made crystal clear. But he had a vision for the kind of life he'd *like* to have and, even more important, he had discovered the beginnings of enough faith in himself— in his ability to become the man he wanted to be—that he'd found a kernel of hope.

And damn if hope wasn't one of the most powerful forces he'd ever experienced.

Didn't mean he wasn't terrified within an inch of his life of fucking it all up. Because he was. After Joss had sent him away that night, he'd walked through the next few days sure a Humvee had taken up permanent residence on his chest. He'd replayed their conversation in his mind over and again, turning it upside down and inside out. Maybe he was missing the forest for the trees, but his brain had zeroed in on two comments that seemed to justify the tenacity of his hope: her saying there were things she wished she could have, and that it would be so much easier for her if they didn't talk.

Was *he* what she'd been wishing for? You know, if he hadn't proven himself a hothead and a Grade-A coward? She'd been right to the bone on that assessment. And wasn't that just a slap in the ass. Still, there was a part of her that wanted him, that felt the magnetic pull that had first drawn him to her on that sunny September afternoon, that wished things could be different. He would bet his life on it. And, since he couldn't change the past—a bitter pill he was finally learning to swallow—he was determined to apply every part of himself to earning back her trust, to deserving her faith.

Thinking her words into the ground and building them back up again, Brady had come to a realization that had nearly taken him to his knees—he was more afraid of never trying and living a wasteful, regretful life of what-ifs than of failing in a spectacular crash-and-burn.

The question was, how to earn her trust. How to make her see that, this time, he *would* control himself, he would stick. How to make her understand how deeply he needed to be there for her and their child.

The first thing he had to do was honor the requests she'd made and the promises he'd given. Despite the ragged hole in his chest only she could fill, he hadn't talked to her. He hadn't visited. It had taken a reserve of strength he wasn't sure he had, but for her, he found he could be so much more than he'd ever before believed.

So he'd kept his word.

But she never said he couldn't give her gifts.

The fact that she'd kept them, that she hadn't thrown them in his face, dumped them on his doorstep, or told him to cut it the fuck out, made him feel ten feet tall.

Brady had just eaten the last forkful of his eggs when another knock sounded at the door. A pair of fairies fleeced him for four dollars this time. It was the matching dimples they wore that really did him in. He'd caved and given them two dollars each.

At this rate, he was going to be broke by morning.

He brought the whole coin jug downstairs, majorly glad for his habit of dumping his loose change in it at the end of the day.

He was out thirty-five bucks when he saw her for the first time.

He'd been shelling out money to a gorilla when Joss answered her door to another group of trick-or-treaters. It had only been a quick glance as she leaned out her screen door, but damn if it hadn't been like dining on a decadent, fresh-made four-course meal after a lifetime of choking down MREs.

And holy hell did he want more.

The next time a group of kids came to the door, Brady couldn't help but linger when they turned from his porch to go to Joss's. And boy was he glad he did.

The littlest kid in the group hung back from the others, too shy to come forward to get her treat. So Joss walked out to drop the candy in the girl's bucket.

And took Brady's breath away.

She was dressed as a Gypsy. Her hair hung wild and loose and curly, a red scarf knotted around her head. Some sort of a peasant shirt left her creamy shoulders uncovered, while layers of colorful skirts and scarves fell over her curves to her bare feet. She jingled when she moved.

The sound beckoned him.

He was immediately and painfully hard. *Jesus*, he wanted her in every way he could have her.

Thank God the Power Rangers showed up when they did, or he wouldn't have been responsible for his actions.

When he finished dishing out…he didn't even know how much money, his gaze drew immediately toward her house.

She was standing on her stoop looking at him.

Every muscle in his body tensed. For the love of God, she was beautiful, exotic, and utterly desirable.

Ask me. Just say the words. He willed her to hear his thoughts.

Joss dropped her gaze and disappeared into her house.

Disappointment threatened to sink through his gut, but Brady would have none of it. She'd more than met his gaze— he'd bet his life that she'd been struggling over whether to speak to him. Otherwise, why would she have stood there so long?

Adrenaline roared through his veins, had him planning, scheming, strategizing.

A vampire came to the door. Brady dropped coins into his bag. "Hey, vampire dude."

The boy turned back. "Yeah?"

"You been next door yet?" He pointed toward Joss's. The vampire shook his pale head. "Think you could handle a special mission?"

"Like what?"

"Tell the Gypsy next door I think she's pretty."

The boy grimaced. Brady dropped two more dollars in his bag. Shrugging, the vampire said, "Okay."

Brady grinned, freaking loving this plan, and waited, his shoulder holding the screen door open.

The vampire knocked at Joss's place.

A moment later, her gaze cut to his. Her blush felt like the sweetest triumph.

Yesiree.

All of a sudden, he didn't care how much money he spent tonight. Every penny would be worth it.

When the next group arrived, he bribed them to tell her

he hoped she was feeling okay. Then he paid a superhero to tell her Brady thought she was pretty. Again. The scowl that earned him made him laugh harder than he had in weeks.

He sent his next message through a cop who apparently wanted Brady to know he'd gotten his money's worth, since he nearly shouted at Joss that if she needed anything, she was supposed to let that guy next door know.

She leaned in to the kid's ear and he nodded. When the boy returned to Brady's stoop, he couldn't restrain himself from smiling like an idiot.

Fuckin' A. They were talking.

The cop eyeballed him for a minute. "She said to say you're a pita. Isn't that bread? Why'd she call you bread?"

Chuckling, Brady dropped another dollar in the kid's bag. "Don't worry about it. Thanks for the message."

He had the next two messengers tell her she was pretty.

He could feel the volcanic eruption brewing through the wall. And he couldn't fucking wait.

He kept it up the rest of the evening. After he'd run out of quarters, he'd gotten to the point of giving the kids big handfuls of loose change to make up for the fact that it was mostly pennies, nickels, and dimes. He'd probably gone through two hundred dollars in change, and he'd never spent better money in his life. When the late hour stopped the kids from coming, Brady battled back his disappointment that the night was dwindling to an end.

His gut told him they'd turned a corner tonight. He didn't know what it meant or what would happen next, but he could be patient. For her.

Brady stood at the kitchen sink washing the grimy feel of the coins off his hands when a knock sounded at the storm door. He grabbed the near-empty coin jug and jogged back to the door.

Two teenagers in jeans and T-shirts stood on the other side.

"What are you two supposed to be?"

The guy grimaced. He wore a spiky pompadour that appeared to have lost a battle with a bottle of gel. And, was it Brady's imagination, or were his eyes yellow?

The girl grinned. "We're Edward and Bella."

Brady frowned. "Who's that?"

The boy blushed at the same time the girl issued a long-suffering sigh. "From *Twilight*," she said in the same tone kids used to say, *well, duh*.

"Uh, if you say so. Anyway, here you go." He upended his jug over the boy's bag and gave them every bit of money he had left. Maybe he should've fished the buttons and pocket lint out of there first.

"Thanks," the girl said enthusiastically. From behind her bag, she produced an envelope. "We're supposed to give this to you."

"Thanks." Brady bolted inside, locked his door, and stared at the envelope for a long moment. Finally, he sat on the couch and ran his finger under the sealed flap to open it. He pulled two pieces of paper out. The first was a note from Joss. Brady ran his finger over the cursive lettering, feeling like he could almost touch her through the looping strokes.

Brady—

Thank you for the gifts. I thought maybe it was my turn.

~J

Smiling, Brady shuffled the note card behind the next sheet.

The breath caught in his suddenly closed throat. His heart thundered in his ears.

It was an ultrasound picture.

Brady leaned in. His gaze traced over every grainy detail of his son or daughter. *So small. So, so small.*

Brady was out his front door before he'd even thought to move. All he knew was that something so inconceivably small *needed him*. Needed his protection. And so did the incredible woman carrying him in her belly.

He stopped before he reached her stoop. Her door was closed, porch light off. In fact, it didn't appear any lights were on in the first floor at all. He took a few steps back so he could see her bedroom windows. A dim light cast a golden glow there.

Didn't she realize he would want to see her, to talk to her, after receiving this picture?

Fine. Baby steps. If that's what she could handle, it's what he would give her. No matter how deep he had to dig to find the patience she required.

He glanced at her room again and imagined her in that cozy space, stretched out on her bed, Gypsy costume cast away on the floor. He wanted her so damn bad.

Forcing himself to be patient, Brady retreated to his place. He cleaned up his dinner mess. Watched a show on TV. Got ready for bed. Everywhere he went, he kept the ultrasound with him. He couldn't stop looking at it.

Maybe it was stupid, but seeing the picture made it so much more real.

His sat heavily on the edge of his bed. Holy shit, he was

going to be someone's dad. He pressed his palm flat to their shared wall.

Now he just had to figure out what else to do to win over the baby's mom.

• • •

She'd come so, so close to giving in. Seeing him that first time, leaning out his door and staring at her like he was starving for her, had been like stepping into a warm whirlpool after a long time in the cold. And, good God, her memory had done him no justice at all. He was sexier than she'd remembered by a factor of at least, oh, eight thousand. Holy crap.

And then all the little messages… Sweet, funny, and sexy. Lethal combination.

Now, lying in bed and knowing he was just on the other side of the wall above her head, Joss couldn't stop thinking about Brady Scott.

The heat in his eyes. The way his biceps strained the sleeves of his shirt. The way his jeans hung on his hips. And oh, those hips, she knew just how they moved, just what kind of pleasure they were capable of providing.

Geez. She kicked the covers off, baring her legs to the cooler air. She was so freaking horny. Between the weeks without sex, the sex-god soldier who lived next door, and the rush of hormones flooding her system, she was a wet, needy mess.

She slipped her hand down her body, over her sensitive breasts, and underneath the satiny band of her panties.

Come on my tongue, sweetness.

Joss moaned at the memory of his voice. That boy had

one talented tongue. Her fingers circled over her clit, ratcheting up the tension that had been gripping her body all night. "Brady," she rasped.

Recalling his intense gaze, the strength of his body moving over hers, the incredibly satisfying fullness of his cock inside her, Joss slipped a finger inside herself, groaning and lifting her hips.

She drew some of the slickness from inside and circled it over her clit, her fingers flying in tight circles.

A noise—a muffled voice?—sounded on the other side of the wall.

Joss froze, her heart thundering in her chest.

There it was again. What was he doing?

Joss rolled out of bed, debated for a moment, and pressed her ear to the cold plaster wall.

Nothing. Huh.

Then, just as she was about to step away, she heard it again. Brady. Moaning.

Holy shit!

She pressed her ear harder to the wall and closed her eyes to heighten her aural senses.

Don't be ridiculous. That could've been anything.

But she didn't step away. And then she heard it again. And it wasn't just any old moan. It was her freaking name. She would've bet her house savings on it.

Left hand next to her head on the wall, Joss spread her legs and let her hand resume what it had been doing moments before. In her mind's eye, she imagined him stretched out on his bed, golden skin completely naked and damp with perspiration, muscles straining as his hand worked up and down his shaft.

Damn, that's hot.

She pressed her hips forward, seeking out the friction her fingers were only too happy to provide. If this wall weren't here, she'd step through, climb up on top of him, and take his cock deep inside her. She was so wet, her body would welcome him in to the hilt in one slick stroke. Fingers gliding, circling, pressing, she imagined it, felt his heat, smelled his scent, heard his harsh rush of breath.

Energy spiraled through her and concentrated low, low in her belly. Joss moaned Brady's name.

A light thump sounded on the other side of the wall, then, another moaned, "Joss." Another thump, like a hand falling flat against the surface that separated them.

The embarrassment she might've felt flew away from her as her body drove her toward release. Knowing he was only inches away, that he was so very close…

Her orgasm detonated within her. She unleashed a long, low moan and her knees went weak as her body convulsed again and again.

A moment later, Brady grunted out her name on the other side of the wall.

Oh. My. God.

Joss dragged a hand through her hair. *Did we just…? And did he realize?*

"Joss?" came his muffled voice. Yeah, he realized all right.

She pressed her ear in tight again.

"I miss you," Brady said louder. He knocked twice. But Joss didn't knock back.

Chapter Fifteen

The next Saturday, Joss wasn't sure whether to expect another gift. Brady had just sent her the costume a few days before. And now that they'd reached an unspoken state of peaceful coexistence, she didn't know if he'd keep giving them or not.

She should go talk to him. She knew she should. She'd half wondered if he'd come over after she sent him the ultrasound picture the other night, but he hadn't. Then again, she hadn't returned his knock, so she couldn't really blame him. Still, disappointment waged war with appreciation within her. She'd asked him not to talk to her or visit. And he'd been true to his word. Well, unless you counted all the Halloween messages. And the mutual masturbation. Since she hadn't had so much fun in weeks, though, she could hardly be mad at him for those.

Finally, she couldn't *not* look out her front door.

A small blue cooler sat on the bricks.

Dying of curiosity, Joss brought it inside and sat it on the kitchen counter. She opened the lid and burst out laughing. Pickles and ice cream. She lifted out the jar of dill pickles, and then the half gallon of french vanilla. Given her milkshake cravings, which had only gotten worse, he couldn't have known just how perfect this gift was. That it was typical Brady smart-ass made it all the more endearing.

After that day, Joss began noting the passage of time and the progression of her pregnancy by the gifts that appeared at her front door. Week 12: A stuffed bear wearing a "Go Army!" sweater. Week 13: A long-sleeved black T-shirt with hot pink lettering over the stomach that said, "Look what my daddy did." She hadn't been able to decide whether to fall over laughing or get pissed at that one, especially when she pulled the shirt out of the box and found another one, a baby onesie that read, "My daddy wears combat boots." Every time she thought of the picture of the big combat boots next to the tiny baby sneakers, she burst into completely ridiculous, hormone-driven tears.

If she didn't count Halloween, Joss hadn't talked to Brady in almost two months, and yet these presents made her feel more and more like he was right here with her. And he was, wasn't he? That was the point. All she had to do was ask him for more, and he was prepared to give it.

So, why didn't she do it?

The question stayed on her mind the whole busy week leading up to Thanksgiving. With less than four weeks until the center's fund-raiser, she was finalizing venue details, making a hard push on selling admission and raffle tickets, and playing on everyone's holiday spirit to beat last-minute donations out of the bushes.

Still, the question nagged at her. And so did the answer.

She was, in fact, falling in love with her baby's father.

And it made her even more afraid.

If she stayed away, maybe this time she could keep from getting hurt. Ever since she'd given Brady the ultrasound, she'd been resolved that he deserved to know his child and play whatever role in his life he could. But if she opened up and let Brady in and it all fell apart, she didn't think she could stand a lifetime of having to see him and pretend her heart wasn't in pieces in her chest.

She wasn't proud of her fear, but there it was.

Since Thanksgiving morning, Brady's truck had been gone, so she didn't bother to check her porch when she got up on Saturday. Instead, she threw herself into baking. She couldn't decide between cinnamon rolls and pumpkin bread, so she made both.

Baked goods heal all wounds. Or, at least, they didn't hurt. Plus, she was damn hungry all the freaking time.

Finally, she had the dishes done and the buns and bread cooling on a rack. She was just drying her hands when a knock sounded at the door.

She tossed the dish towel over her shoulder and answered. For a moment, her brain couldn't place the familiar woman standing on the other side, and then she gasped.

"Hi, Joss," Brady's sister rushed to say. "I'm Alyssa, Brady's—"

"I remember. Of course." Joss scrambled to organize her thoughts. "Wait. Did Brady send you?"

Alyssa shifted her feet. "No. Not at all. In fact...do you think I could come in?"

"Sure." Joss stepped back and let Alyssa pass. She took

a mental inventory of her appearance, wondering if Alyssa would be able to perceive the tiny baby bump under her yoga pants and tee. Alyssa turned, relief apparent on her face, and suddenly Joss knew. "He doesn't know you're here, does he?"

Alyssa twisted her lips and shook her head. "No, but I really wanted to see you. I'm sorry I've just barged in here unannounced. I didn't know how else to contact you."

"Okay, well, do you want a cup of tea?"

"I'd love one."

Joss fixed the tea—decaf for herself now that the baby was on the way—and plated a few cinnamon rolls. She set the table for the impromptu chat and invited Alyssa to sit.

"I really like how you've decorated. All the color makes it so warm and inviting," Alyssa said, stirring cream and sugar into her tea.

"Thanks." Joss passed her the buns and then took one for herself, not sure exactly what to say.

Alyssa sat back in her chair. "I'm sorry this is so awkward. Maybe…can I just be totally forward and ask you a question?"

Joss gave her a small smile. She liked her all the more for just diving right in, so she decided not to make her ask. "Yes, I'm pregnant. And yes, it's Brady's." Alyssa's jaw dropped. Joss's stomach followed. "Oh, God. That wasn't the question you were going to ask?"

"Actually, it was. But between Marco and Brady, I'm not used to someone who just cuts to the chase without a lot of hemming and hawing."

Joss sagged in her chair. "Oh, thank God."

Alyssa chuckled. It was contagious.

"How far along are you?" Alyssa asked.

"Fourteen weeks."

"Have…um, have you guys talked about it?"

Joss tilted her head and looked at the younger woman. "Can I ask why you're asking me and not him?"

Her cheeks went pink. "I'm, uh, not exactly supposed to know. Yet."

Alyssa's comment raised so many questions in Joss's mind she didn't know how to feel about the fact that Brady hadn't told his sister.

"I overheard the guys talking on Thanksgiving Day. They thought they were being all stealthy, but honestly they're nowhere near as sneaky as they think." She shook her head. "Anyway, that night, Marco told me. Well, more like, I forced it out of him. I guess Brady told him a while ago and asked him not to say anything to me until he'd had a chance to talk to you. But I know Brady and I doubt he's done that. And Marco told me..." Alyssa shifted in her seat. "He said Brady didn't handle it well when you told him about the baby. And I've been worried about you, so…"

Joss's heart gave a squeeze. Bad enough she might be in love with Brady, but every minute she spent with Alyssa, she liked her even more. *She could be your sister-in-law*. Joss choked on the sip of tea she'd just taken. Where the hell did that come from?

"I don't know what to say," Joss finally managed.

Alyssa met her gaze. Her eyes were so like Brady's, it made her miss him even more. "Was it really bad?"

She didn't have to ask what Alyssa meant. "Yeah. He did try to talk to me, though. Later. You should know I'm the one who wouldn't agree to a relationship."

His sister gasped. "He wanted a relationship?"

Joss was taken aback by the sheer surprise in Alyssa's tone. "I think so. I didn't really let him get that far." She sighed. "Listen, you might as well know something about me. I was orphaned when I was a little kid. I barely remember my mother. And I spent most of the time until I went to college in a children's home. Given all that, I don't have a lot of tolerance for risk. And, well, your brother — "

"Seems like a risk? Trust me, I know. But we have more in common than you might think."

Joss finished her tea and debated, then finally said, "Go on."

"Our mother died when I was twelve. Brady had just turned seventeen. It destroyed our dad. Within months, he subsisted pretty much on vodka alone. He was angry at the world and he took it out on us. Well, mostly on Brady."

Goose bumps erupted on Joss's skin. "Oh, my God. I'm so sorry."

"Brady became my de facto parent after that. When he graduated high school, he refused to go off to college and leave me. Instead, he got an apartment and moved me in with him. And he put his life on hold for almost five years until I graduated high school and went to college." Alyssa sat forward. The love she felt for her brother was evident in her tone, in her expression. Joss's throat tightened when she imagined a much younger Brady dealing with such an impossible situation. "I'm telling you this because I want you to know that he *can* commit, he can be a great caregiver. He and Marco are the most selfless people I've ever known. I don't know where I'd be without them." She wrapped her arms around herself.

"What he did was very admirable," Joss said, her mind struggling to process.

"But you're not convinced."

"I don't know. A sister is forever, you know? He has been trying to show me, though." The words were out of her mouth before she'd thought them through.

Alyssa's eyes went wide. "What do you mean?"

Joss debated for a long moment, then pushed from the table. "I'll show you. Come upstairs with me?" Alyssa's obvious enthusiasm made Joss very curious to see what she'd make of the gifts.

She turned into her office and flipped on the light switch. She lifted a box onto the desk chair and, one by one, laid the items out onto the desk—the book, the costume, the shirts, the bear. As she did, she told Alyssa about the other gifts he'd given her, too.

When Joss looked up, Alyssa's eyes were glassy.

"Oh," she said. "He…" She nodded. "He's really trying." She grabbed Joss's hand. "Whatever happens between the two of you, if you'll let me, I'd like to be there for you. I'd like to be an aunt to this little one. The two of us, we don't really have any family—well, except for Marco and his parents. So I… But only if you—"

Joss squeezed her hand. "I'd like that."

Back downstairs, her head spun with emotion while Alyssa insisted on helping clean up the dining room. "So, what do you do for a living?" the other woman asked as she settled a stack of dishes into the sink.

"I'm the assistant director of a children's community center. You?"

"I'm an event coordinator at the Washington Convention

Center."

"Wow."

"Well, a *junior* event coordinator. I've only been there four months."

"Still, I bet that's exciting. What's the coolest event you've been involved with so far?"

Alyssa paused in front of the stove. "Hmm. Latin Fashion Week was a lot of fun. I also worked the Washington Bridal Showcase. That was great considering I was just starting to think about the wedding. Oh, and we have a professional boxing event about once a month. I'm the JEC on that event now."

"Professional boxers, huh?"

Alyssa grinned. "Uh huh."

Joss chuckled. "Must be such a hardship."

She laughed. "Yes, yes it is. But it's a sacrifice I'm willing to make."

"I bet. An event planner. Well, I should pick your brain sometime. My center holds an annual holiday fund-raiser event for the huge parts of our budget not covered by county funds. There's a band, lots of really good food, and we do live and silent auctions, a toy drive, raffles." She shrugged.

"Oh, yeah? I'd be happy to help if I can."

They exchanged phone numbers and e-mail addresses. Joss promised to send her materials about the center's event, and Alyssa suggested they brainstorm over lunch after she'd had a chance to read through everything. They made a date.

Alyssa slipped her coat on and paused at the door. "I'm really glad I came, Joss."

"Me too. Thank you for doing it. I'm sure it wasn't easy knocking on a stranger's door."

She smiled. "Weird thing is, you don't feel like a stranger." Her cheeks colored at the admission.

"I couldn't agree more."

Alyssa's smile faded. "I don't want to pressure you, but I think you need to know something. Oh, maybe I shouldn't." She shook her head and looked to the ground.

"Well, now you sorta have to," Joss said.

"Was afraid of that." Alyssa gave her a small smile. "Okay, then, here goes. I don't think this excuses anything, but it might help you to know that the night you told Brady about the baby, well, Marco and I had just left not long before. We'd just learned that our father died."

The words sank into Joss's brain and the hair raised on her neck and arms. *It's all ruined now.* The memory of his anguished voice flooded chills through her despite the thick T-shirt she wore. "The funeral," Joss whispered. "The night he came to see me, after that, he said he'd been at a funeral."

"Yeah. Please think about talking to him?"

Alyssa gave her a hug and they said their good-byes. Joss stood at the door until she pulled out of the lot.

Afterward, she sat on the couch and thought about what Alyssa had said. The night she'd gone to him, Brady was grappling with the news of the death of his abusive father.

"Oh," she said, tears springing to her eyes as his voice played in her head again. *I am not a victim,* he'd said before. "Oh, Brady." Fat tears rolled down her cheeks as the pieces fell into place.

Suddenly, she was on emotional overload. Sympathy for what he'd gone through. Guilt for not giving him a chance. Fierce appreciation for Alyssa's courage in coming here, telling her, giving her more than a little hope and understanding.

Amid all those, another emotion stood out the most. Love.

The emotion slammed into her with such certainty she felt plastered to the couch, like gravity's pull had suddenly multiplied.

She was in love with Brady Scott.

Now she just had to figure out how to tell him.

• • •

Knock, knock.

Brady's eyes whipped open. He listened, not sure if he'd heard something or dreamed it. A few hours before, he'd gotten home from spending Thanksgiving at the Vieris' and the weekend at Marco and Alyssa's place. He'd collapsed on his bed after a long run and a hot shower, not intending to fall asleep. Apparently, his eyeballs had other plans.

Knock, knock.

Louder. The sound was louder. And he'd definitely heard it. He flew into a sitting position and stared at the wall.

Warm pressure filled the space around his rapidly beating heart. Was this finally happening? Was she was really knocking for him, after all this time?

He stretched his arm around the headboard of the bed and returned the greeting. He held his breath and listened. The sound came back to him again.

The next instant, Brady was off the bed and tugging on clothes. Jeans. T-shirt. Boots. Socks and boxers were luxuries he didn't make the time for.

He pounded down the stairs, heart in his throat, and flew out the front door.

He stopped short. Joss was crossing the sidewalk to him.

She froze, tugging the lapels of her coat tighter to her throat against the crisp, early December night air.

His jaw dropped open at the sight of her. Long hair lifting and curling by the cold breeze. Eyes shining in the lamplight along the sidewalk. Jesus, he'd missed her so damn much.

"Hi," she finally said.

She'd come to him. She'd talked to him. It was more than he could take. He couldn't hold back what he felt anymore.

In two long strides he was right in front of her, wrapping her in his arms, pulling her in tight against his body. He kissed her temple. "Hi," he managed.

Her body began to shake. She pressed her face into his chest.

"Hey. Hey, now. Don't cry." He stroked her hair over and over. Her tears gutted him, but he'd take every bit of it, for her.

"I'm sorry," they said at the same time.

Brady pulled back and tilted her chin upward. "What on earth would you have to apologize for?"

"I was wrong to try to exclude you from the baby." Her teeth chattered.

Her words sank into the depths of him, warming, healing, strengthening. He could stand out here all night and never feel the season's bite. But she couldn't. "You're freezing. Will you come in?"

She nodded. "I'd like that."

He tucked her against his body and led them into his house. Her shoulders relaxed within his grasp as the indoor heat surrounded them. "Can I take your coat?"

"Sure," she said.

He slipped it off her shoulders and she unwound a pink scarf from her neck that matched the colorful strands of her hair. Then she turned around.

Brady did a double take. She wore the T-shirt he'd given her, the one that proclaimed his role in…her no-longer-flat abdomen. A small swell pushed out the bottom of the shirt. He tossed the coat to the chair and stepped toward her. He reached out, then quickly withdrew his hand and lifted his gaze to hers.

She pulled his hand back and placed it on her belly.

Awe. Sheer and total. It was the only word he had for the emotions that flooded through him as he touched her for the first time in months and his child for the first time ever.

The breath caught in his throat. He looked into Joss's bright-green eyes and so many things competed to be said at once that he said nothing at all.

Hand still on her stomach, he came closer. Swallowing hard, he finally said, "I can't tell you how much I've missed you."

"Me, too."

"You had every right to keep me away."

She shook her head. "No, I didn't. But fear makes you do the stupidest things. I'm sorry."

"That's the damn truth. But, much as I appreciate your apology, don't be sorry. If I hadn't acted the way I did, maybe you wouldn't have been so scared. You had every right to protect yourself. And this baby."

Needing to touch her more, touch her everywhere, Brady reached to cup her face in his hand. He stopped just shy of making contact, not sure what she'd allow, what she wanted. She leaned her face the rest of the way into his palm.

It slayed him.

He closed his eyes, afraid of how much emotion he might release through his gaze, and lowered his forehead to hers. For long minutes, they stood there together, just holding each other.

It was possible he had never in his life been more at peace.

Her fist curled into his shirt, and he knew he was wrong. That simple expression of need felt like she'd reached into his chest and soothed the ache that had surrounded his heart.

She tilted her head back, bringing their faces so close together her soft breath caressed his lips. "What you said, do you still feel that? I'd understand if—"

"That I've fallen in love with you? Yes, Joss."

She sucked in a breath and chewed at the corner of her lip.

He cupped both hands around her face, holding her to him. Heart thundering against his breastbone, he spoke words he never thought he'd hear himself say. "I love you."

Her eyes went glassy and her lip trembled. "You do?"

"Yes. Even before the night…" He swallowed the lump of regret in his throat. "That night, I'd just learned my father died. To say we had a difficult relationship would be a mild way of putting it. I'd been planning to confront him. I was *so* angry at him. And I thought I needed him to take that turmoil away. So when he died, I thought, 'That's it, there goes my chance.' I couldn't be with you with all this rage inside me. When you came that night, as much as anything else, I was mourning the loss of any chance with you."

"I'm sorry," she whispered.

He shook his head. "None of this excuses what I did. I just want you to know I'm working like hell to square myself away and become a better man. For myself. For you." He glanced down between them. "For the three of us. God, I love you."

Joss nodded. "I…I…"

He wanted the words as much as he needed his next draw of air. But only when she was ready. Only when she meant them the way he did. So he kissed her, just a light brush of lips. "You don't have to say anything. Just the fact that you're here is enough."

She gave him a small, shaky smile. "What now?"

"Would you stay the night with me? I don't think I could stand to let you go right now. I just want to fall asleep with you in my arms and wake up next to you."

Joss's whole face lit up, and he felt her happiness down deep. What he wouldn't do to put that look on her face every day of her life. "I'd like that."

Brady shut out the downstairs lights and returned to her. He laced his fingers into hers and guided her up the stairs and into his bedroom.

He pulled back the covers and kicked off his boots, then he turned to find her expression full of emotions. His gaze followed the line of hers to the ultrasound picture he kept in a frame on his nightstand.

"I came to see you that night. To thank you."

Her lips dropped into an oval. "You did?"

Brady nodded. "I turned back at the last minute. You'd asked me not to come over. I didn't want to mess up, especially after you'd spoken to me that night. Well, had the cop speak to me. He wanted to know why you were calling me bread, by the way."

Joss's grin turned into a chuckle. "You totally were a PITA.

But it was fun. Classic sailor boy." She winked.

Brady shook his head and laughed, actually glad for her to be giving him shit. "I liked what happened later that night even more."

Her cheeks went pink, but she chuckled. "Yeah, that part was pretty nice, too."

He grinned, climbed into bed, and patted the space beside him.

She settled in next to him on her back. When she licked her lips, the silver of her piercing flashed at him.

The humor melted away in favor of fierce need to taste her. To run his hands over her soft bare skin. To bury himself deep within her tight heat. God, it had been so long.

But he didn't want to scare her. He didn't want to rush her. And he sure as hell didn't want her to think the only thing he wanted was sex.

Brady shoved his arousal back a few good steps and stroked the hair off her face. He caressed her arm and traced over her fingers. His gaze landed on her belly. He slid his hand where his eyes were looking. So hard to believe his child grew inside her.

Meeting her gaze, his fingers traveled to the hem of her shirt. "Can I lift this, just a little?"

Joss tucked one arm behind her head and nodded.

Brady tugged her shirt up until the soft skin of her stomach was free. Joss hooked her thumb in the stretchy pants she wore and pushed the waistband down an inch or two, baring her whole abdomen to his gaze.

Gently, he dropped his palm to her skin. Lying on her back, the bump wasn't as pronounced, but he *knew* what was there. He pushed himself down the bed until his face was level with her stomach.

Hey little dude. I'm your dad. I'm going to try really hard not to be an asshole. And to stop cussing. I'll probably suck at both. But your mom is totally awesome so it'll all be okay.

Joss's breath caught. Brady glanced up. "You won't suck at being a father, Brady."

He'd said that out loud? *Shit.* His cheeks went hot. "I really hope not. I'm going to try so hard, Joss." He pushed up on an elbow, met her gaze, and dropped a kiss to her belly.

Her eyes went glassy and she smiled.

Brady kissed every part of her bump, needing his hands and lips on her, needing her peach scent in his lungs, her softness easing his hardness.

Joss shifted her legs. "Brady."

He turned to her, the tone of her voice beckoning. Her mouth hung open. Her chest rose and fell quickly. The green of her eyes scorched him.

Instantly, his body was right there with her. He shook his head. "I wasn't trying to—"

"I know. But I've really missed you."

"Jesus, Joss. Are you sure? I don't want you to think I only—"

"Don't you want to? Anymore?"

The uncertainty in her voice hauled him up to her. He kissed her mouth, his cock punching against his jeans. "I ache I want you so much. I will always want you. Don't you ever question it."

"Okay," she whispered.

"I just want you to be sure. I don't want you to…regret anything." The memory of the last time he'd used that word with her stuck in his throat like a shard of glass.

She traced her fingertip over his brow, down his temple, across his cheek, like maybe she was memorizing the contours of his face. "Brady, you're going to make mistakes. And I'm going to make mistakes. You know? We don't have to be perfect at this. So, I'm sure. I want you."

The breath rushed from his chest. "I want you, too. So much."

Their clothes came off in a rush, Joss's surprised laughter at his lack of boxers filling his chest with a healing warmth.

"You know what I just realized?" Joss asked.

"What's that, sweetness?" He pressed a lingering kiss over her heart.

"We finally made it to a bed." She grinned.

"Yeah. We did. And that means I finally get to take my time with you." Brady's brain filled with plans and desires. He scooted her into the center of the bed and sat on his knees between her legs.

He massaged her feet, her calves, her thighs. And then he started over again at her toes with kisses. He treated her belly to another round of worship before working his way up to her breasts. He kissed and licked and sucked her nipples into his mouth, reveling in every single one of Joss's moans and squirms.

He cupped a breast in his hand and feathered his thumb over her nipple. "These are bigger," he said, kissing her again and waggling his eyebrows like a cartoon villain.

Joss rolled her eyes but laughed. "See, there's a silver lining after all."

He dragged his body over hers, aligning their gazes. "You're the silver lining, Joss. That I actually get to have a chance with someone like you. And that you're giving me the family I never thought I'd have. That's the silver lining."

She wrapped her arms around his neck. "Make love to me."

The words settled into every cell in Brady's body, re-making him, or making him better, for her. "God, yes."

He lowered his weight to her body, but held himself up on his elbows. His cock nestled against the soft hair and en-ticing heat between her legs. He rocked himself against her, grinding the steel of his length into the nerves at the top of her sex. She gasped and moved her hips in time with his movements, her knees drawing up, her thighs falling open.

"Brady," she rasped. "You're going to make me come."

He smiled down at her. "Good."

"I want to come with you in me."

Her words washed every bit of his willpower right down the drain. He drew his hips back, aligning himself. Then he sank into her, inch by slow, deep inch.

"Fuuuck." He groaned, overwhelmed by how good she felt. How good he felt with her. "Wrap your legs around me."

Her arms and legs came around him, holding, comfort-ing. He grasped her shoulders for leverage as he worked himself in and out of her tight, slick heat. He rolled his hips, grinding against her clit and then sinking deep before pull-ing almost all the way out again. It was torturous and so damn good. The way she clung to him. The way she breathed his name. The way she made him believe again.

"I love you," he whispered against her temple.

She gasped and then she was holding her breath, her body tightening around his.

"God, yes, sweetness. Give it to me." His strokes moved harder, faster.

Her head reared back into the mattress, her mouth dropped open, and she moaned, long and low, her body squeezing him like a fist over and over again.

Brady snapped. He hooked an arm under one of her knees, opening her farther, and chased down the end of the storm roiling through his body.

"Oh, oh, fuck. *Joss*," he groaned, his orgasm nailing him in the back and forcing him into her in an unrelenting series of quick, deep strokes. Even after he'd spilled his release, he continued to move, softly, reverently. Despite the force of his orgasm, he was mostly hard within her.

She gave him a warm, affectionate smile and ran her hands over him.

Jesus. Is this what it's like? Is this how it feels for everyone? He dropped a kiss to her forehead, the corner of her eye. "I never want it to end, Joss."

"It doesn't have to."

He captured her mouth with his, sealing the promise between them. She had given him so much—a chance at peace and happiness, a family, herself. Well, everything but the words. Maybe he shouldn't want them as badly as he did. But he felt the weight of passing time acutely. Every day they remained apart was one day closer to the end of his stateside tour. And now that he had her in his arms again, he wanted it *all*, with her. Still, he'd have to be patient. He *could* be patient. For her.

Finally he withdrew and laid his long frame tight against the side of her body. He might've dozed off for a while when she roused him to go to the bathroom. They redressed, him in boxers and her in her T-shirt and panties, and climbed under the covers in the quiet darkness.

He pulled her back against his front, tucking his knees up against her thighs and his hand around her belly.

"Know what I was wondering?" he asked.

"No, what?"

"How did you know the trivia about my dog tags? That first day."

She chuckled. "It wasn't as impressive as it seemed. Military recruiters give presentations at the center several times a year. Some of our kids enlist because they can't afford to go straight to college. I've gotten to know some of them and picked a few things up."

"Hmm. Know what else I wondered?"

"Nope," she said, humor in her voice.

"Why 'courage'?"

"Oh. It's an E.E. Cummings quote. 'It takes courage to grow up and become who you really are.' I first read it in eighth grade. It always helped me remember to be who *I* was, and not who other people thought or wanted me to be. I got that tattoo right before my freshman year of college. I was finally on my own, and I didn't want to forget."

Fierce admiration of her flowed through him. "Are you the birds?" He kissed her back.

"Yes," she said quietly.

"And did they find their freedom?"

Joss gasped and turned her head toward Brady. "How did you know that?"

"My childhood wasn't great either," he said.

She kissed him and settled back into the pillow. "Did you find *your* freedom, Brady?"

Soul-deep certainty made him squeeze her. "I have, now."

They were quiet for a long moment. He wondered if

she'd fallen asleep. "Hey, I have an idea," came her soft, tired voice.

He nuzzled against her neck. "What's that?"

"Want to go on a date with me?"

He chuckled. "We kinda went about this ass-backward, didn't we?"

"Maybe a little. So?"

"Let me think about it. Umm, yes." She elbowed him, and he kissed her cheek. "You just name it, sweetness. And I'll be there."

Chapter Sixteen

Joss spent every non-working moment of the next three weeks with Brady. True to his word, he'd agreed to everything she suggested, and he even planned a couple dates himself. They went to the movies and discovered a common love of action flicks and thrillers. On nights when she didn't have him over for dinner—she loved cooking for him—they took turns introducing favorite restaurants to each other. They went into the city for the lighting of the National Christmas Tree and stood wrapped around each other near the fire as they listened to the carolers sing. And Brady even accompanied her on some of the evening errands she had to run to pick up donations for the auctions.

When she met Alyssa for lunch to discuss the fund-raiser, she suggested they both bring the guys along. She and Aly had taken turns telling the story of the day they'd talked. Joss had worried that Brady would be upset with one or both of them, but the moved look of appreciation he'd worn as he thanked Alyssa was a sight Joss would never forget.

The only thing that had detracted from their intense, whirlwind time together in the slightest was Joss's inability to verbally express her feelings for him.

She was so frustrated with herself. She knew how she felt—she loved him. It wasn't even a question. And she was just totally amazed at how expressive and open he'd been with her ever since the night of their reunion.

That night, she'd still been too scared to actually say what she felt. And then she'd been so overwhelmed by his devotion and attention. And every day since that had passed made it harder to say the words. The weight of not saying them closed off her throat every time she tried to speak. She'd totally psyched herself out and couldn't get unpsyched.

Brady showed her nothing but acceptance and appreciation. He deserved the same from her. He deserved the words.

As she dressed for the center's holiday fund-raiser, Joss resolved to tell him tonight. For the past week, he'd thrown himself into selling admission and raffle tickets, and even gathered a few last-minute items for the silent auction. Some of the guys from his office would be attending the party, and she was looking forward to the opportunity to get to meet them.

Her front door opened and closed. "Joss?" Brady called, his keys jingling.

"I'm upstairs. Can you help me?"

He jogged up the steps.

She got in a good, long ogle of him in his dress uniform. Damn, the boy cleaned up good. "You look very nice."

He grinned. "Ah, the uniform works for you, does it?"

She chuckled. "Always. I can't wait to see it on the floor later."

"How important is this party again?" Brady pushed his hips into hers. "Because I can be convinced to keep you in bed all night long."

Smiling, she turned in the circle of his arms and made sure her bottom brushed against his erection. He groaned. "Very. Now, would you zip me up?"

She had managed to find a beautiful ivory gown with an empire waist that flattered her growing figure. The scoop neck and elbow-length sleeves gave it a vintage feel she loved, so she'd had her hair done earlier in the day in a classic updo that created surprising twists of pink within the dark brown.

Dragging his finger up her spine, Brady slowly zipped her gown. "Stay right there," he said. A moment later, his hands came in front of her and settled a chain against her throat.

"Brady," she gasped. "What did you do?"

He hooked the clasp and kissed her neck. "It reminded me of the pink in your hair."

Joss stepped into the bathroom, her gaze immediately drawn to the sparkling emerald-cut pink sapphire. "Oh, my God. It's gorgeous, Brady. Thank you. I can't believe you did this."

His gaze met hers in the mirror. He shrugged. "You look beautiful."

She turned and kissed him, *the words* pinging around inside her like a pinball.

"Ready to go?" he asked, offering her his arm.

He drove them to the luxury hotel where the event was being held, and Joss thanked the weather gods that the flurrying earlier in the day hadn't turned into full-on snow-storm. She didn't want anything to prevent the event from being a huge success for the center.

The banquet room hosting the event was beautifully festive. Of its own accord, the hotel decorated the room with a mammoth, ceiling-high Christmas tree in the center of the room and smaller but equally elaborately decorated trees in the corners. Thickly ornamented evergreen garland hung across every doorway. At one end of the long room stood rows upon rows of silent auction tables, and a few early birds moved up and down between them and added their names to the clipboards to bid on the more than one hundred fifty items she'd managed to collect. A stage dominated the other end of the room and the band played lively holiday music. A lavish buffet of entrees and desserts ran along one wall, and tables filled the middle of the space. Near the central tree sat a huge red velvet chair for Santa, wrapped gifts piled on each side.

Why is the chair empty? Where is Santa?

Joss turned to Brady. "I need to find Nina. Come with me?"

He kissed her hand. "Of course."

"Hi, Miss Joss," came again and again from a few of the center's kids who had already arrived. They got to come to the party for free thanks to the hotel's generosity. Center families also received reduced ticket prices. It was a night out unlike what many of the kids ever had the chance to experience otherwise, and Joss loved seeing the girls in their velvet and taffeta dresses and the boys with their hair combed down and wearing ties each year.

She said quick hellos to each of the children and greeted

their parents, promising to catch up with them again during the party.

"Finally," she said as she spotted her director, Nina Johnson, huddled in the corner with Christina and a hotel manager. She joined them and made introductions. "Have we heard from Santa? He's not here yet."

Nina frowned. "Santa canceled a half hour ago. The flu."

Joss's stomach sank to her toes. "What are we going to do?"

"Javier has been making some calls for us, but it's Saturday night two weeks before Christmas."

Javier tilted his head, sympathy warming his eyes. "I have not been able to find another available Santa."

"Brady," a voice called. Both he and Joss turned. Alyssa and Marco were crossing the room.

"I'll be right back," he said.

Joss nodded. "We have to have a Santa. That's the highlight for the kids." She looked over her shoulder to see Brady standing with Alyssa, Marco, and several men she didn't know.

"Would you like me to keep trying?" Javier asked. "Perhaps a costume rental shop would have a Santa suit available and you could find a volunteer?"

Joss and Nina exchanged glances and they both nodded. "Yes, please, keep trying," Nina said. "And checking on a Santa suit would be a great Plan B."

"I'll get right on it. You have my number if you need me before I check back in." Javier gave a quick bow and departed through a service door.

"Don't panic," Nina said. "People are just starting to arrive. We have time to figure something out. A little, anyway."

"Something will work out," she said, willing herself to

believe her own words. Brady waved Joss over to his group of work friends, judging by the impressive collection of military dress uniforms. With Brady stood two more army guys and one marine.

He grasped her hand and pulled her next to him. "Gentlemen, this is Joss Daniels. Joss, this is Victor Keith, Danny Fernandez, and Bobby West." She shook each of their hands in turn and said hello. "This man right here," Brady said with a big smile as he clapped Bobby's shoulder, "is your unlikely looking elf for the evening."

"What do you mean?" she asked, trying to focus on the conversation while worry squeezed her gut.

"Bobby works with the Toys for Tots program."

"Oh, that's wonderful. Some of our families apply to it. But what does—"

"I understand you're in need of a Santa suit," Bobby said.

She gasped. "You have one?"

"I know someone who does. It's on its way."

She squealed and hugged Bobby. "You totally are my elf. I'm going to find a way to thank you for this."

Bobby grinned. "No need, ma'am. I'm glad I can help."

She turned to Brady. "Thank you," she said. "I don't know what I'd do without you."

He smiled and Joss could swear his chest puffed up. "I'll hang here with the guys and we'll keep an eye out for the suit to arrive. I'll find you as soon as it does. So go do the things you need to do and don't worry."

"Okay. I will. Thank you. Oh, where did Alyssa and Marco go?"

"Looking at the silent auction, I think."

Joss nodded and pushed onto tiptoes to give Brady a

quick kiss. He caught her shoulders and held her a moment longer. She pulled away laughing. Then she ran to tell Nina the good news and see what other fires might need putting out.

•••

Brady emerged from a stall in the men's bathroom. "Don't say a word."

Bobby, Victor, and Danny all burst out laughing.

"Yes, Sergeant Santa," Victor chortled.

Brady glared and turned toward the mirror. *Aw, hell.* The Santa suit had arrived, and Brady'd had a momentary lapse in cognitive function wherein he decided it would make the most sense if he donned the costume and saved Joss the stress of finding a volunteer. But now…

"I'm the least convincing Santa there ever was," he said.

Bobby tried not to laugh but failed. "Put this on next," he said, handing him a big furry blob. The beard. Elastic bands looped around his ears. The mustache was attached and filled with wire that could be shaped over the lip. Next came the wig. Brady settled it over his head, which was easy since his hair was so short. Finally, Bobby handed him the cap and a pair of wire-rimmed glasses filled with fake lenses.

"Uh, we have a problem," Brady said. His dark eyebrows now stuck out like a pair of inchworms crawling across his forehead.

Bobby held up a tube. "We have a solution." He uncapped it and leaned in.

"What in the hell?" Brady grumbled, glaring at Victor and Danny as they stretched to watch Bobby work.

"There. Look."

Brady turned back to the mirror. "Huh." Whatever the stick was had turned his eyebrows white. In a not *too* fake way. "You have a Santa belly for me in that bag of tricks?"

Something pillow-like whacked him in the gut.

"Asshole," he said, chuckling.

Danny elbowed Victor. "I don't think that's approved vocabulary for Santa."

"Keep it up. Wait 'til you see what's in your stocking this year."

"That's the spirit," Victor said.

Bobby helped stuff and organize his belly and buckle the wide black belt. "There."

Not bad. Not bad at all. He turned to the guys. "How do I look?"

Danny's expression cracked first. "Like someone who is thoroughly pussy-whipped." Bobby most tried to resist, but then he joined the others, who were laughing so hard they could barely remain upright.

Ignoring the asswipes behind him, he fished his wallet and a few other necessities from his uniform pants and slipped them inside the pocket at his hip. Luckily the coat and all the padding would hide the lump. "Whatever. You three be dickheads all you want. I make this shit look good. I'm outta here."

"Wait," Bobby choked. "Don't forget your bag. These are the favors for the kids."

"Fine."

"Maybe you should…practice your ho, ho, ho. You know, to…make sure it's authentic," Victor said, nearly wheezing.

Brady threw the bag over his shoulder. "Ho, ho, fuck

you." He stalked out of the bathroom, and could still hear their laughter at the far end of the hall.

• • •

A commotion erupted at the doors. Joss turned and relief flooded through her veins at the sight of Santa Claus arriving. *Wonder who it is?* Had Brady's friend found her a volunteer, too? She was going to have to find out the guy's favorite beer and send him a whole case.

She made her way across the room to give New Santa the instructions Flu Santa had received in advance. Nina beat her to it. Her director joined New Santa's side and began whispering to him even as kids came running up to him. Joss grinned. New Santa saved Christmas for the center's children. She might just have to give him a kiss for that.

She backtracked through the room to the stage and cued the emcee. He made a big welcome announcement and then the band seamlessly segued into "Here Comes Santa Claus." Applause and cheers sounded through the room.

The kids lined up for Santa and in a time-honored tradition took turns sitting on his lap. Each child received a hearty "Ho, ho, ho" and a colorful ribboned bag from Santa's big red sack.

"This party is awesome, Joss," Alyssa said, coming up beside her.

"It really is, especially with Santa here. Look how excited the kids are," Marco added.

"I know. I'm so relieved." She turned to Alyssa. "You look gorgeous, by the way." Brady's sister wore a strapless bright red sheath dress. Sparkly silver shoes peaked out from under the hem.

"Thanks. So do you. I think you just might be glowing." Alyssa grinned.

Joss could almost believe it. She was happier than she could ever remember being. She smoothed a hand over her belly.

"So where's Brady?" Marco asked.

"I don't know. He was going to watch out for the Santa suit to arrive. But I haven't seen him since." She scanned the room and shrugged. "I'll find him. You guys should get something to eat."

"What about you?" Alyssa asked.

"I will. Later. My insides feel like Jell-O right now." Between the Santa mishap, general stress over wanting the party to be a success, and hoping to find the perfect moment to finally give voice to her feelings, no way she was chancing food.

She glanced around the room, still not finding Brady in the crowd. "Would you excuse me? I'm going to try calling him."

"Don't worry." Marco smiled. "He won't have gone far from you."

"I know." And she did. Brady knew how important this night was to her. He'd already proven that by getting his friend to save the day. She threaded her way through the minglers to the lobby outside the ballroom and tried Brady's number. It went right to voice mail.

Victor and Danny rounded the corner, beers in hand.

She stepped into their path. "Hi. Have you seen Brady lately?"

They glanced at each other. "No. No, uh, he came to find you," Danny said.

Joss narrowed her gaze. Danny was acting squirrelly. "Seriously. Where is he?"

"He went in the ballroom," Victor said.

She sighed and glanced back into the crowd. Including the center's children, there were about three hundred guests. She'd find him eventually. She just hated for him to feel she'd worked all night and ignored him.

Nina found her a short time later. "Ready to be the hostess with the mostess?" she asked.

"Absolutely."

Nina wrapped arms with her as they walked to the side of the stage. They stepped up onto the platform and waited for the emcee to introduce them. Joss used the slightly higher vantage point to search for Brady again. She was half tempted to ask the emcee to call his name. Not that she would. But where the hell was he? Exasperation had morphed into worry that had boiled into a healthy dose of *I'm-gonna-kick-me-some-sailor-boy-butt!*

"Ladies and gentlemen, please offer a warm round of applause for your hostesses this evening, the community center's director, Nina Johnson, and assistant director, Joss Daniels."

Applause drew them to the center of the stage. Nina offered some general welcoming remarks and talked a little about the services the center provided. "Now, we have some very good news to share with you tonight." She smiled at Joss. "But before we get to that, let me take just a final moment to recognize the tireless service of my assistant director, Joss Daniels, who planned just about every part of tonight's event. Didn't she do a wonderful job?"

Applause and cheers of "Go, Miss Joss" filled the room.

Joss stepped up to the microphone. "Thank you. But I enjoy this event far too much to call it a job. I hope you're enjoying it, too." The crowd applauded again. Joss gave a wave, her stomach giving a little squeeze. What was Nina's good news?

Nina held up an envelope. "I've received word of how much we brought in in ticket sales and donations, so far. And I'm happy to report, we've broken a record."

Joss gasped as butterflies flittered through her abdomen. She pressed a hand to her belly to ease the nervous twinges.

Nina made a big show of sliding the card from the envelope. You could feel the anticipation tingle in the air.

"Through the generosity of everyone in this room, from tickets and donations alone, so far we have raised $21,500."

The audience whooped and hollered.

Now, if that didn't make the night merry she didn't know what did. Tears pricked at Joss's eyes. Her mouth dropped open as she looked at Nina to see if she'd really heard what she thought she'd heard. The most they'd ever made from this part of the event was $12,000. The auctions were always the real moneymakers.

Nina raised her hands to quiet the cheers. "But the night is young. And those tables over there are loaded with items and experiences you're going to want to fight to have. So everyone go bid, go raise your bids, and have a—"

Joss sucked in a shocked breath and grabbed her side. Something spasmed in her stomach. Down low and to the right.

Nina turned to her. "Are you all right?"

Brady was instantly on his feet and weaving his way through

the crowd, trying not to push or make a scene but desperate to know what was wrong. Jesus. Was it the baby?

Joss's laughter rang out through the PA system. "I'm sorry. The baby just kicked for the first time. I think he was going for a field goal." Her voice was full of such happiness. "I also think he heartily approves of the incredible generosity of spirit you've all shown here tonight."

Laughter and applause filled the room.

It took a moment for the meaning of her words to sink into Brady's brain. Then he almost went to his knees. Adrenaline carried him to the stage as the crowd started to disperse and mingle again.

"Santa, is everything okay?" Nina asked.

Still smiling and holding her belly, Joss glanced down at him. Her green eyes went wide. "Bra— Santa?" She surveyed those closest to the stage, presumably looking for kids who might've heard her revealing his true identity. She knelt near the edge of the stage. "What are you—"

Heart thundering in his chest, Brady couldn't stand for even that much space to separate them. He slid his hands under her arms and swung her down off the low staging. She gasped and gripped his shoulders. Hugging her into him, he said, "You scared me. I thought—"

"I'm sorry. I didn't mean to." She pulled back. "Brady, you have to feel this."

He pressed his palm to her belly. Waited. He met her gaze, alive with excitement.

Kick. Kickkick.

His jaw dropped. "That's him?" It was the most amazing thing he'd ever experienced in his life. Everything about Joss and the baby filled him with awe.

She grasped his face through the beard. "I can't believe *you're* Santa. I've been looking for you for an hour, at least." She smiled. "I can't believe you did this." She waved at the costume. "But thank you for doing it. It means so much to the kids. And to me. You were my hero tonight." Tears filled her eyes and her bottom lip trembled. "I love you so much, Brady."

The room narrowed to the two of them. His heart leapt to his throat. *Did she just—*

"I do. I love you. I'm sorry I couldn't say it before. I was just—"

Brady tugged the beard free of his mouth and kissed her.

Murmurs filled the ballroom around them. He knew he'd broken character, but no way he could hold back from claiming this woman a single second longer.

"Miss Joss is kissing Santa Claus!" a little girl's voice called out.

The room erupted in laughter. The band didn't miss a beat and broke into "I Saw Mommy Kissing Santa Claus." The crowd starting singing along.

Joss's eyes popped open wide. They laughed into the kiss.

She'd finally given him the words. He'd been waiting for weeks. For forever. And now that's *exactly* what he wanted. Time was too short. Already a part of him was worried about what happened eighteen months from now. In the meantime, he didn't want to waste a minute with her.

Brady reached into his Santa suit pocket and grasped the little leather box there.

He opened it and dropped to one knee.

Joss's face bore the most beautiful, open expression of surprise. "Brady?"

He nodded and focused his whole heart on her. It was

easy. She owned it completely. "You have given me things I never thought I could have. Taught me things about myself I didn't think I could learn. And made me happier than I ever thought I could be. You ease me, and I don't want to spend another minute without you by my side. Joss Daniels, would you do me the greatest honor of my life and become my wife?"

"You…you want me…?" A tear spilled from each eye as she left the question hanging there.

"Oh, sweetness. I'll always want you."

Her smile was pure joy. "I'll always want you, too. So, yes, Brady. Yes."

He rose from his knee and swept her off her high heels. He let out a loud whoop that received a huge, raucous round of applause. Joss threw her head back and laughed. Next to that "yes," it was the most beautiful sound he'd ever heard.

He settled her back on her feet and grasped her left hand. The ring had an emerald-cut diamond and rows of diamonds inlaid in the band. But what had drawn him to it was the antique look of the setting. It was her. He slid it on her ring finger. Then he pressed his lips to the very same spot.

She gazed down at the ring, eyes alive with excitement. "It's stunning, Brady. And just perfect. All of it." She gently pulled the Santa hat and hair from his head.

"But the kids."

She chuckled. "I think they have a pretty good idea that I'm not Mrs. Claus."

"Mrs. Scott sounds better, anyway." Smiling, Brady tugged her to him and dipped her back. Grabbing his arms, she squealed and broke into a deep belly laugh. And then he kissed her long and hard, marveling at how the rest of his life had started with just one night.

Epilogue

"You look so stunning," Christina said, adjusting the comb that held the veil in the back of Joss's hair. "I'm so happy for you."

"I'm really happy for me, too. Sometimes, it's hard to believe this is really my life," Joss said, turning to the mirror. And it was true. If someone had told her a year ago that today she'd have a child, a husband, and the confidence in herself and her relationships to know it would all last, that she was wanted, she never would've believed it. "I'm ready." She smoothed her hands over her long white gown.

Dressed in a beautiful golden dress, Alyssa stepped next to her and squeezed her hand. "I couldn't be happier to be getting you for a sister. And what you've done for Brady, the peace he's found with you, there just aren't words to tell you how much his happiness means to me."

"I know. I feel the same way about you." Joss squeezed back. "And, Brady, well, he makes me just as happy."

"What do you say, Alyssa? Is it time we take this girl to join the wives' club?" Christina smiled.

"Definitely." Alyssa grinned. She and Marco had married the first weekend in May. It had been the quintessential beautiful spring day, and the mountain lake setting they chose for the ceremony was simply breathtaking. The only thing that didn't go according to plan was Joss going into labor in the middle of the reception.

Nicholas Andrew Scott—a tribute to the man who had always been, and continued to be, like a father to Brady—was born twenty-four hours later on May 5th.

How he'd gotten to be almost four months old already, Joss didn't know. Time was moving so fast, too fast.

"All right," she said, reaching for her bouquet. "Let's go get me a husband."

Joss followed her best friends out of the hotel suite they'd stayed in the previous night and down the hall. They'd come back to the same hotel where Brady had proposed to her last Christmas. It held so many special memories for the both of them. This was the place where she'd conquered her fear and declared her love for him, the place where he'd made it clear he wanted her, forever. So it had just seemed right.

Finally they arrived at the doors to the same ballroom, divided in half to make the ceremony space more intimate.

A year ago tonight, Joss had met Brady at the park as she waited for the fireworks to begin. What if he'd never come back with their dinner? What if she'd told him he couldn't sit down? What if she hadn't offered him that one night together? She couldn't imagine her life without Nicky, without Brady, without the new extended family she'd found in the Vieris. Alyssa, Marco, Lily, and Nick had all vowed to be there to support and help Joss and Nicky when Brady was deployed again next summer. But it would just be for one year. One year and then he was out, retiring—a decision he'd come to on his own. Joss never would've asked him to change who he was for her, but Brady said he needed to change who he was for himself.

So, yeah, crazy as it had all seemed at the time, that night had been the first night of the rest of her life. She released a deep breath and pushed all the thoughts away. She wanted to be here, totally present in the moment, because she didn't want to miss a single minute of her new life with Brady.

The doors to the ballroom opened and the music began. Christina went first. Then Alyssa. Joss moved into the opening and looked to the front of the room.

Brady stepped forward, handsome and sexy and tempting as usual in his dress uniform.

Beside him, Marco held Nicky in his arms. She adored that their son could be a part of this day. And the baby tuxedo was too cute for words.

Brady smiled, his gaze beckoning her to come to him.

She couldn't resist him. She'd *never* been able to resist him. Thank God for that. So she took one step, then another, then another. And it was exactly how they'd make this new life—one neither of them ever expected to have—work. One step at a time, one day at a time, one night at a time. With love and trust and faith full in her heart, Joss went to the man who had become her partner, her protector, her biggest hero, knowing he wanted her as much as she wanted him. And always would.

Acknowledgments

I have so many thanks to offer for this book. First, to Heather Howland, for always believing in me and my stories. Thank you for this wonderful partnership we have. Second, to authors Christi Barth and Joya Fields, for offering me your comments on the manuscript and helping me make it so much better. Third, to my family, for always supporting my dream. And finally, to the readers. Sometimes, characters really stick with you, and that's definitely been the case with Marco, Alyssa, Brady, and Joss. So I'm thrilled and so appreciative that you all have embraced these characters and helped me bring their world to life. I have the best readers *evah!* ~LK

About the Author

New York Times and USA TODAY bestselling author Laura Kaye has written nearly a dozen books in contemporary and paranormal romance. She grew up amid family lore involving angels, ghosts, and evil-eye curses, cementing her lifelong fascination with the supernatural and storytelling. Laura lives in Maryland with her husband, two daughters, and cute-but-bad dog, and appreciates her view of the Chesapeake Bay every day.

www.LauraKayeAuthor.com

Manufactured by Amazon.ca
Bolton, ON